(ng

CW00549300

RUSSIAN ROULETTE

The
Konstantin
Files

Keith Nixon

Fiction aimed at the heart
and the head...

Published by Caffeine Nights Publishing 2014

Copyright © Keith Nixon 2014

Keith Nixon has asserted his right under the Copyright, Designs and
Patents Act 1998 to be identified as the author of this work

Published in Great Britain by Caffeine Nights Publishing

www.caffeine-nights.com

British Library Cataloguing in Publication Data.
A CIP catalogue record for this book is available from the British
Library

ISBN: 978-1-907565-98-4

Cover design by
Mark (Wills) Williams

Everything else by
Default, Luck and Accident

Acknowledgements

Dream Land
For my children
William, Florence & Tabitha

Plastic Fantastic
For Nick Horne, the real Nikos
A great friend, who never shies away from telling you
exactly how it is…

Fat Gary
For Tony Black
Top bloke, top writer

Bullet
For Al Kunz
The Big Boss at Books & Pals
Thanks for giving me the chance

Infidelity
For Ryan Bracha
Martin Stanley
Mark Wilson
Three of my favourite indies

Close Contact
For Rich D
Martial Arts Master

A Chorus of Bells
For Darren Laws
Caffeine Knight

Praise for Russian Roulette

'If you told me that Konstantin put the K in KGB, I wouldn't even argue. This character is a badass of the highest calibre.'

Gerard Brennan, author of *Undercover*.

'*Russian Roulette*, Keith Nixon's fast-paced collection of seven novellas, feels cinematic, like *Snatch* meets a steampunk Sherlock Holmes: deliciously foreign and saturated in the other, offering American audiences a first class seat to see how noir is done across the pond. Navigating an exotic subculture of ecstasy-dealing English toughs, dominatrixes, crime lords, loan sharks and all sorts of lowlifes, Nixon continues the story of Russian-born Konstanin, anti-hero for the modern age. Like Marlowe before him, Konstantin has a penchant for finding trouble—and an unflinching sense of morality to get him out of it.'

Joe Clifford, author of *Lamentation* and *Junkie Love*.

'Nixon delivers a series of hard-edged twists and turns that will leave you reeling and turning the pages in what is an unforgettable story.'

Richard Godwin, author of *Hitman* and *One Lost Summer*.

'Hardboiled action and sharp, gritty humour. Highly recommended.'

Paul D. Brazill, author of *Guns Of Brixton* and *A Case Of Noir*.

'Flat, monotoned, dreary landscapes against which two of the most original characters ever seen in literature—Konstantin and Fidelity—operate together and separately in linked stories in a series of nourish nightmares that will have you screaming inside your skull. This is what noir is all about. Masterful, deadly and powerful.'

Les Edgerton, author of *The Rapist, The Bitch* and *The Genuine, Imitation, Plastic Kidnapping.*

'If you thought "The Fix" was a blast of black comedy, you ain't seen nothing yet. In this collection of fast-moving novellas, reacquaint yourself with Konstantin Boryakov, a tramp claiming to be ex-KGB. The people who cross him may be sorry, but you won't be.'

Nick Quantrill, author of *The Late Greats.*

Contents

Dream Land

A Cold Welcome

The yellowing bruises on Konstantin Boryakov's face were momentarily invisible, lost in the lurid glow of the amusement arcade called Dreamland.

The many coloured light bulbs flashed and flickered even at this hour. It was very late, or maybe it was very early. Whatever. Inside him was darkness and, behind, waves repetitively beat at the sea wall.

A road stood between Konstantin and the amusement arcade. No traffic. Well, there had been a single car, but it made itself scarce moments ago around a corner after depositing Konstantin on the kerb.

He looked at the piece of paper in his palm, an address scrawled in crabby handwriting upon it. Red pen. No idea where the place was. Neither had the driver.

A quick glance in both directions revealed a single person in sight. A man with an unsteady gait. He weaved. Left, right, forwards, backwards. Like he was walking into a gale.

Drunk.

Konstantin sighed. Didn't like dealing with the inebriated. They were unpredictable. Neither was he in the mood. Jetlagged from the flight, angry at the driver for dumping him here, worn down after months of confinement. Russian prisons were hard places. His ribs hurt, unfit after being confined for weeks on end, body battered from repeated 'persuasion techniques'. But they'd learnt nothing. And now Konstantin was somewhere in England, some time in 1995, 1,500 miles away from Moscow, the FSB and the Lubyanka prison. Even the borrowed clothes still itched his skin. But he'd no choice.

"Hey. Excuse me," he said.

The drunk paused, lifted his eyes from the pavement to Konstantin's face, struggled to focus.

"What you want, my man?"

Konstantin held out the paper, said, "Where this place?" Too tired to bother smothering his Russian accent.

The drunk's eyes widened, head lolled from side to side, body swayed.

"Dunno."

Konstantin stepped closer, could taste the stench of alcohol bleeding out the man's pores. Lifted the address right in front of his face. Waited while the pupils found their range, took a while.

"Oh yeah. I know there."

"Tell me."

"Once you've handed over your wallet, mate." A new voice, from behind.

The drunk shrugged, shambled past Konstantin.

He turned slowly, saw three men arranged in a semi-circle, spaced out, Konstantin at the locus. Cursed himself, lost his edge when he'd been inside. No way would these punks have sneaked up on him six months ago.

"What if say no?" Konstantin wanted to see the reaction, measure the opposition.

The one in the middle, the leader, laughed. Flashed a knife. Confident, despite being significantly shorter and slimmer than Konstantin. Arrogance in numbers. Good.

"Just give us your wallet and your bag, you'll be fine."

"Dave, he sounds like one a' them Eastern Europeans, them bastids that're nicking our jobs, like."

The guy on the left. Fat, acne scarred, many times busted nose. A failed boxer in other words. The one on the right, tall and skinny with a twitch, stayed silent.

"Where you from, mate?" Dave the Rave said, ignored the fact that he wasn't a local either, had moved down from London. To claim the dole while living by the sea. Since then sold a bit of gear to make ends meet. Used a bit too much of it himself though. A couple of sandwiches short of a picnic.

"I not your mate," Konstantin replied.

"Yeah, that's true, which is why you're going to take a good leathering before we take your stuff."

"Who first?"

Dave laughed. "Peaches, have him. Should be a piece of piss for you."

It transpired Peaches was the ex-boxer. He stepped forward, right leg leading, fists up in loose balls. Konstantin waited for him to near, skipped forward, kicked a heel out, struck Peaches on the knee, heard it rupture.

Peaches' mouth fell open, verbally paused as if the assault hadn't really happened, then the reaction from his nerve endings hit. Brain first, mouth next. Let out an ear-splitting scream. Hit the deck hard, writhed like a landed fish, grasping his damaged limb. Konstantin ignored him, was out of the game.

"Now that weren't nice you Polack bastard," Dave said, brought the knife out into full view, weaved the blade as if attempting hypnosis.

"I Russian," said Konstantin.

"Whatever," said Dave.

The skinny one hefted his weapon, a broken pool cue. Four feet long, jagged end where the tip had been sheared off previously. Clearly fancied himself as some sort of Jedi Knight, the way he flourished it.

Konstantin ignored the weapons, focused on Dave's eyes. Waited for the flicker.

Saw it.

Moved before Dave, closed the gap faster than the smaller man expected and was inside his reach as the knife began its swing. Konstantin grabbed his forearm with both hands, spun Dave around, twisted behind his back and up. The knife fell to the floor, spun like a roulette wheel. But no luck for Dave tonight.

Held short of snapping the arm like a branch as Skinny finally swung the pool cue in a wide arc intended to take Konstantin's head off. But he ducked and the lump of wood smacked into Dave's skull, cut off the scream before it even emerged. Dave slumped to the pavement, like a crumpled heap of rags.

For a moment Skinny stared open mouthed at his fallen leader, realised he'd fucked up and needed to make it right. Pivoted the cue back over his head in an executioner's stance, wielding an axe. Brought it down.

The cue smacked harmlessly into Konstantin's palm, held it for a moment as Skinny struggled. Smiled. Then punched him full in the face with a massive left fist. Skinny went out like a shattered light bulb.

Konstantin tossed the cue over the wall, picked up Dave's knife and stuck it inside his jacket. Searched both unconscious forms. A few ten pound notes in Skinny's jacket, but a thick wad on Dave, accompanied by a large bag of drugs. Pocketed the cash, poured the wraps down the nearest drain.

But he still had a problem.

Walked over to where Peaches was rolling from side to side, whimpering. Konstantin held up the piece of paper, now stained with blood, in front of the man's eyes.

"Tell me where this is or bust other knee."

Peaches told.

A Matter of Life and Death

Dave the Rave felt like the side of his face had been hit by a truck.

He gingerly peeled his eyelids back, felt the beginnings of a bastard sized headache coming on. Looked slowly around. Neither Skinny, nor his trusty cue, was anywhere to be seen. Peaches lay flat out ten feet away, face down. Appeared like he'd tried to crawl away, passed out with the pain.

Stood up, took about half an hour to get to his feet. Knew immediately there was something wrong. His jacket felt light. The knife he wasn't bothered about, could nick one of those from any supermarket. It was the money and the drugs. He'd only just got the stash, sold hardly any. Owed his dealer big time for it.

Dave checked every pocket three times, a sense of dread throttling his heart further each occasion his hands came up empty. Looked around frantically in case they'd fallen out in the heroic struggle. Got on all fours, crawled every inch of the pavement.

After a couple of minutes Dave discovered the bag in the gutter. Led him to the drain, oblivious to the stench wafting up. Could see the wraps floating on the turgid fluid below. He tugged at the metal grate, wouldn't budge no matter how hard he tried.

Dave began to cry, knew he was probably dead now. Deliberated for a minute whether to run or ring. Decided on the most sensible option. He wiped the salty tears away, pulled out his phone, tapped in a number. Connected.

"Do you know what time it is?" the voice heavy with fags, booze and threat.

"I've been mugged."

"You what?" said Frank McGavin, Dave's dealer.

"Got caught out by a couple of guys. They've had the merchandise away."

"So?"

"I just thought you should know."

"Makes no odds to me, Rave. You've got a line of credit for another 48 hours. Then it's my cash or your head. Simple choice."

"But the drugs are gone!"

"As I said, not my problem. Two days. Maybe less if I'm feeling really miserable."

Dave opened his mouth, but would only be speaking to static.

Two days. What the fuck was he going to do?

Considered running again.

A Bit Of Charlie

Konstantin waited for the lift to arrive. Heard it clank way up the shaft, cables straining as it sank downwards. Questioned for a moment whether to take the stairs. Then decided not to. Wasn't strong enough.

The doors opened, revealed a small metal cube. Graffiti covered, piss smeared. Stank. Reminded Konstantin of the cell he'd recently vacated. He couldn't bring himself to step inside. The lift waited patiently for thirty seconds, then decided to shut up shop.

Konstantin jagged out a hand, halted the doors in their tracks. Retraced their steps with a squeak, got stuck three-quarters open. He stepped inside, pressed the button for the floor he wanted. Didn't like it, not easy to escape from a high rise. Wondered why this had been arranged as a safe house. It looked anything but.

The cables took the strain, began to slowly, painfully, haul Konstantin up. It was hot in the confined space, made the stench of urine worse. The acrid odour caught the back of his throat. He was used to smelling his own expulsions, didn't appreciate that of others.

After an eternity the lift shuddered to a halt, doors squealed, stuck again. He slid through, bag in hand. Onto a landing, corridor, doors – some numbered, most not. Konstantin looked for the one he wanted, banged on it hard. Felt pain in his knuckles where he'd hit Skinny. For a moment Konstantin couldn't believe he was here, trying to access some run-down place to lay his head.

Nothing. Hammered again. Eventually heard movement within, locks unfastened, chain rattled, bolts slid back. The door opened a crack, an eye there. Bloodshot. Smell of sweet, herbal smoke and alcohol.

"What?" A hard voice, scraped through with a couple of tonnes of gravel.

"I sent by Lamb."

A sigh. "Ah bollocks."

The door closed, but not completely. Konstantin heard the chain drop, opened up again, wide. A short man stood in the entrance. Stained vest, baggy trousers, unshaven but bald. Several double chins, hairy shoulders and a greasy sneer.

"You're not what I expected," he said.

Konstantin shrugged, didn't give a shit. Entered, pushed past him. Got a whiff of stale body odour.

The Russian combed the flat. Scrutinised the narrow corridor, small bathroom, two bedrooms and a living room.

The resident took the search with bad grace. Konstantin ignored it. Finally dropped his bag on the floor. Stared through his reflection in the large window that looked out over the sea. Lights on the water. Knew they were large container ships heading in and out of the Thames.

"What your name?" he asked.

"Charlie," scratched an armpit, looked like a monkey suffering the onset of alopecia. "Look, how long you going to be here for?"

"I not know."

"Well that ain't really good enough."

"Not my problem. Lamb said you debt to repay. This it. You not like, talk to him."

Konstantin watched the emotions skitter across Charlie's face as he thought through his situation and possible consequences. Fear dominated. Mr. Lamb was not a man to cross.

"Okay. But not for long. All right?"

"I need sleep."

"Your bed's back here."

Charlie led Konstantin back along the corridor, pointed into a box room filled with junk and a stained mattress. The Russian exited, went to the other bedroom.

"No, this mine."

"It fucking ain't!"

Konstantin swivelled his gaze onto Charlie. Shut the door in his face.

He sat on the bed, which sagged almost to the floor. Tired, but not from lack of sleep. He'd never felt so alone in his life. He was totally on his own now. Cast out, adrift and with only one immediate purpose in life. Someone he had to see. But she couldn't be allowed to spot Konstantin, because he was dead.

But after that? He didn't know.

Stayed awake for a couple of hours until the sun rose.

Distinguishing Marks

Konstantin stood under the miniscule trickle of water that was supposed to be a shower. It was one of those electric efforts. A couple of settings, including one that read 'Power'. Not a word he'd have selected. 'Slightly improved dribble' was more appropriate. The bathroom was as cold as a fridge, mouldy as mature cheese.

He washed off the soap suds, the bar an ancient chunk as durable as rock. But Konstantin didn't care, he'd been living in his own excrement for months.

For a moment he was back in the Lubyanka. Where most of the time he existed side by side with his own filth, hadn't seen a toothbrush for weeks on end. Got washed off by the guards periodically when the smell got too much. So frankly, this was paradise.

A quick towelling dry, didn't bother to shave. Thought he might try out a beard.

Konstantin stepped into the corridor, naked. Ignored the initially surly, then embarrassed, Charlie leaning against the wall, waiting to enter his own bathroom. He scuttled inside, slammed the door.

Konstantin smiled, enjoyed irritating the other man. Hoped he'd had an uncomfortable night's sleep. He got dressed again in his same borrowed clothes. Decided he needed to appropriate a new set. Tugged several bank notes from a thick pile which he subsequently hid. He expected Charlie would be going through his possessions as soon as his back was turned, so left some of the wad he'd taken from Dave in the bag.

Five minutes later and the Russian was outside in the early morning sunlight. The granite grey apartment block was to his back. It appeared a walk to his right would take him into town.

The streets were bereft of people. Plenty of seagulls though. Noisy, big bastards with beady eyes that were merrily ripping rubbish bags apart and spreading rotting waste across swathes of the pavement. Scavengers. The lepers of avian society. Konstantin took an instant dislike to them.

He walked the area for an hour. Past the amusement arcade, dim now in the sunlight, and funfair. The rides were silent, gates locked.

Into the shopping centre. Poorly built from cheap materials, mostly charity shops.

To the old town, which had a little more class, but had seen better days.

Onto the jetty which created a protective harbour for a few fishing boats. Konstantin could see the rotting stumps of what had once been a pier jutting up from the water.

Up the hill past the police station, a place to avoid in the future, and the Winter Gardens sunk into the chalk.

Kept walking along the cliff edge until the houses petered out, then returned through the maze of narrow streets filled with terraced residences.

Konstantin felt surprisingly at home, liked the seedy, jaded atmosphere. The rough edge, the tired buildings, slight feeling of menace. It was his sort of place.

People were stirring now. Curtains began to twitch, windows thrown wide open to allow cooler air to enter the house where previously they'd been closed to refuse access to intruders.

Konstantin was aware he couldn't delay it any longer. Knew really he shouldn't be going at all. Nevertheless hailed a taxi, gave the man the address seared into his memory.

Sat back. Dreamt.

Old Wounds

"Stop here," said Konstantin.

The driver pulled into the kerb. Said, "£3.20 mate."

"Wait please."

"It'll cost you, mate."

"No problem." Konstantin wondered whether everyone around here referred to each other on such personal terms. If they did indeed, actually all know each other.

The address was just a few doors away on the other side of the road. A large, detached house in a relatively pleasant area, the sea just a matter of yards away. The driver turned the engine off and immediately the temperature began to rise inside.

Konstantin was itching to get out, go and ring the bell, but knew it was the last thing he could do. He was supposed to be a corpse. Had to stay that way. He caught a movement, curtains being opened. Saw the woman, hard to tell from this distance, but he was sure she looked just a little older. Blonde hair pulled back into a ponytail like always. White top on. That was it.

He sat there for another ten minutes. The driver laid his head back on his seat, nodded off. Began to snore. The meter ticked upwards. Now double the cost. Konstantin didn't care. Then the front door opened. A girl stepped out. Tall, light brown hair, pulled back into the same style as her mother's. She wore a grey school uniform. Konstantin merged with the shadows. Watched her walk along the road.

He pulled out a creased ten pound note. Dropped it on the man's lap. Got out, left the car door slightly ajar.

Began to follow the girl.

A Chance For Redemption

Dave was at the hospital, more accurately, Accident and Emergency, accompanying Peaches. As a busted knee wasn't considered life threatening Peaches occupied a wheelchair in the waiting area with a handful of others. All lingering interminably.

"Here you go, mate," Dave said and handed over a cup of weak tea issued forth by a vending machine. A scum floated on top, but Peaches seemed not to notice. His face was creased in a permanent frown of pain.

"Wish the bloody docs would get a move on," he said. "Feels like I've been here hours."

"That's the trouble with the NHS," Dave replied. His coffee tasted no better than the tea looked. "All them foreigners clogging the system up."

Peaches snorted, said, "Don't get me started."

"You seen anyone yet?"

"Some nurse just after I arrived. Said I was a low priority."

They sat in silence for a few minutes, watched a woman in a washed-out blue uniform behind a thick piece of glass tap away at a computer.

Probably playing games, Dave thought.

"Good of you to keep me company," said Peaches.

"Well, I'm not really here for that."

"Oh."

"Yeah, it's a warning really. We're in trouble."

"What kind of trouble?"

"The deep shit sort. My drug dealer. Frank McGavin."

If there was any blood left in Peaches' face, it drained out there and then. Dave could hear the dry gulp, saw the hand shake, spilled the tea. Which was probably a blessing.

"What we done?"

"That bloke we sorted out this morning. He had the drugs. Frank wants paying."

Peaches crossed his brows, thought hard. Was like watching a cow cram itself through the eye of a needle. Slow and difficult.

"But, Dave. Them weren't my drugs. They was yours."

"Yeah, but Frank knows you're my mate. He might come and see you. Put the squeeze on."

"I'll tell him I know nothing."

Dave shook his head, said, "Won't mean a thing. He's a killer that one, cold as a gravestone."

"So what we going to do?" whined Peaches.

"Find the Polish bastard. Do him over. Give him to Frank."

"I thought he was Russian."

""Polish, Russian, they're all the same."

"Will it work?"

Dave wasn't so sure, but said, "Like a wet dream Peaches. We just gotta find him."

"I think I know where he is."

Dave couldn't quite believe his ears. Ran the words through his mind again. Still couldn't. Felt his heart leap like a salmon, powered by wild hope. "You what?"

"He showed me an address."

Dave gaped. Wrung out, "Where?"

"Arlington House."

"Peaches, you fucking beauty."

"What number?"

Peaches stayed silent. Dave repeated himself.

"Dunno."

The salmon of hope came crashing down again.

Then Peaches said, "But I do remember what floor he's on."

A couple of hours later they were out on the street. Dave on his two feet, Peaches on two wheels.

"Got a pen?" said Dave.

"Why?" said Peaches.

"I want to be the first to sign your leg," said Dave and rapped on the cast that now encased Peaches' knee.

Open All Hours

Konstantin nursed a beer. Already sunk three in short order, barely touched the sides despite having not eaten since yesterday lunchtime. Melancholy fed him.

He'd followed the girl at a gentle amble. Hugged the shoreline, spent most of her time with face angled to the sea, enjoying the breeze on her skin. Retraced his steps past Dreamland, the high rise and to the train station. The girl met a friend there, garbed in an identical uniform. The pair hugged, kissed each cheek, giggled about something. They headed onto a platform, talked incessantly until the train arrived. Clambered on and headed west.

Konstantin stood staring at the tracks for a long time. Two other trains came and went. Eventually he shook himself mentally, shambled aimlessly. Found he was in the Old Town, saw a pub open at a ridiculous time in the morning. It was surprisingly busy. Old soaks outside smoking, older soaks inside topping themselves up with liquid amnesia.

The Russian settled in immediately, no one questioned his presence. Seemed nobody wanted to. His morose attitude covered him like a shroud. Made him invisible, like the rest of them. Decided he'd get very, very drunk.

Then maybe hit somebody quite hard.

Target Acquired

Dave and Peaches spent hours banging on doors in Arlington House, floor 6. Some answered, most didn't. Peaches had better success, the wheelchair and cast probably disarming residents. But they didn't find the Polish guy. Or the Russian either.

At last Peaches dropped his bombshell, said, "Maybe it was floor 5?" As Dave's face took on an interesting colour, Peaches scrambled an explanation to save himself. "They do look similar!"

Dave considered throwing Peaches off the flats, wheelchair and all. The height would definitely kill him. But remembered he still needed the bastard. Took several deep breaths, calmed down. Called the lift to descend. Let Peaches take the stairs.

They hit paydirt within fifteen minutes. An overweight bloke in a stained vest several sizes too small opened his door to the temporary cripple. When he confirmed to Peaches he knew a Russian, Dave appeared. Shoved him backwards into the flat. Produced a yelp.

"Charlie," said the guy with the vest when Dave asked his name. Surly, aggressive. That was okay, Dave could do the same.

"Got here early this morning, did he?" asked Dave.

"Might have done, what's it to you?" Suddenly defensive, wary.

"Know Frank McGavin?"

"Yeah, doesn't everyone?"

"Well, we work for him and he wants this guy."

Got a shrug from Charlie.

"Says he'll deal with anyone who gets in the way. Personally. So you gonna help me or not?"

"This is where he slept," said Charlie, suddenly going out of his way to be cooperative. "And that's his stuff."

Dave went through the large canvas holdall, dumped everything out on the bed. Grimaced. Other than his knife there was nothing of any value, no sign where he'd come from or gone.

"What's this crap?" asked Dave, holding up an extraordinarily heavy, green-ish coat. Several dubious stains on the outside and the inside.

Charlie shook his head. Didn't know.

"Well, when he comes back be sure to give me a ring." Handed over a number.

"What's in it for me?" asked Charlie.

"Survival."

Dave the Rave wheeled Peaches out to the lift. Felt like he had a glimmer of opportunity. Just had to wait now. He hoped it wouldn't be long.

Because tomorrow Frank would come calling for his money.

Or his head.

Super Tramp

The air hit him hard. Like walking into a wall. Suddenly Konstantin felt utterly hammered. He'd got fed up with beer, didn't like the volume, so switched to vodka. Pretty much drank the bar dry. Or the landlord had hidden the rest to get rid of him.

Whatever. Time to move on anyway.

He had no idea where he was. Just wandered aimlessly. Everything was hazy. As if he was looking at the picture on a television screen when the aerial wasn't quite aligned right. His legs felt tired so he sat down. In the entrance to a store. Windows boarded up.

A moment later the sun was blotted out. Someone said, "You're in my spot."

Looked up, struggled to focus. Saw a badly dressed man, hair everywhere. Gloves and a coat, even in this weather. Smelt him too. A homeless person.

"I said, you're in my spot. Are you going to shift it or shall I do it for you?" A lot more aggression in the tone. Palms crushed into fists.

"Sorry," mumbled Konstantin, stood up.

"No problem," replied the tramp, suddenly calm, transgression over. Took Konstantin's place, wrapped himself up in a blanket that came out of nowhere. "Look, apologies if I was rude, but you have to protect your patch, you know?"

Konstantin did. More than the tramp appreciated. But he didn't have a patch to protect any more. It had been taken away.

"Want a drink?" the tramp waved a bottle shaped brown paper bag at Konstantin.

"Got my own." Showed vodka, bought from who knew where. Konstantin sat down next to the tramp.

Neither spoke, watched the world go by. Eventually Konstantin noticed a pattern, asked, "Does everyone ignore you?"

"Yes, they try extremely hard not to notice me. It's the closest to invisible a man can get in this day and age."

The Russian liked that idea. Wondered how he could achieve that for himself.

"Then again..." the tramp inclined his head. Konstantin followed the bearing, ended up at a beat copper en route. Sighed.

"You here again, Ralph?" said the constable, nervous smile on his face. Young, barely graduated. Voice largely absent of authority. Probably beaten up regularly at school.

"As you can see Constable Gregory, I am."

"Well, we've spoken about this before, haven't we?"

Gregory was phrasing everything as a question, like he was talking to a child. It was starting to annoy Konstantin.

Ralph stayed calm. "You know I don't like the shelter."

"But you should be there, shouldn't you?" Gregory stretched out an arm, crooked a finger. "Come one. Let's go."

"He said he doesn't want to," growled Konstantin.

The constable switched his attention, said, "And who might you be, sir?"

"His friend."

"Then perhaps you wish to join him at the shelter?"

"No."

Gregory bridled, aware of a couple of people stopping to watch, said, "I'm a police officer, sir. If I tell you you're doing something, you will do it."

That was it. Konstantin was sick of being ordered around by people who thought they knew better, believed they had the authority whether true or not. He rose to his feet, stretched his considerable height above the constable, who suddenly realised the situation he'd put himself in. The colour dropped out of his face like it was tied to a two tonne weight.

The pair of spectators became a small crowd.

"I'm warning you, sir. It's an offence to strike an officer of the law." His voice quailed, but was loud.

Konstantin laughed, said, "I not going to hit you, *little man* You beneath me." Then he belched, loud and lurid, in Gregory's face. The constable began to cough, struggled with the wretched fumes. The gathered shoppers thought this hilarious and burst out laughing. A couple even applauded.

"Ralph, you come with me," said Konstantin, turned his back on Gregory, audience over. "Stay at my place."

"Okay. Give me a moment to gather my things."

Then Gregory did something very stupid. He flicked out his baton, the sound designed to intimidate. Konstantin rotated, smiled at the policeman.

"You not want to do that, my friend."

"Sir, I am arresting you."

"What charge?"

"Vagrancy."

"Ridiculous."

Someone in the crowd, which was reasonably large by now, jeered.

Gregory whispered into his microphone, "Officer needs back up. Urgent. Repeat urgent."

"Pathetic," said Konstantin, waved the wimp in a uniform away. Bent to help Ralph gather his things.

Turned around, felt something acrid hit his face. It burnt. Konstantin dropped Ralph's possessions, clawed at his skull, dropped to his knees.

Heard the words repeated, "Sir, I am arresting you…"

Lost the rest as he sank back into his place of calm, where he had been trained to retreat in times of extreme stress and harm. Didn't hear the bacon van arrive, more coppers pile out, shove him in the back, the click of a lock.

Behind bars. Again.

Mr. Lamb Makes An Appearance

"He's in here."

The sergeant stopped at the cell door. Heavy metal, inset window. He slid it open, peered inside. Satisfied, he unlocked the door, yanked it open. No melodramatic creak, which disappointed Mr. Lamb.

"Five minutes, all right?" said the sergeant.

Mr. Lamb nodded, stepped inside. Heard the clank behind him. Stood over the large form for a moment. Could tell Konstantin was awake. He sat down on the end of the cot, waited. He had as long as he wanted, regardless of what the sergeant believed.

"I thought we not supposed to meet again," Konstantin eventually said.

"And I thought you said you'd keep a low profile. Obscure was the agreement."

Konstantin rolled over, sat up, dropped bare feet to the floor. Twisted his head to bring his eyes, still bloodshot from the mace, on Mr. Lamb.

"Sorry," he said.

"In this case I understand it wasn't entirely your own fault. The Superintendent acknowledges Constable Gregory was being over-zealous. He wasn't supposed to have the spray. They're letting you go."

"Good. Thank you."

Mr. Lamb held up a hand, said, "But he also says you're not welcome here any more."

"This not Wild West."

"Granted, but we don't want anyone checking into your background, do we?"

"No." Said grudgingly.

"I'm sure the Superintendent will give you a couple of days while I sort out where to move you. Provided there's no further trouble."

"Good of him," Konstantin said with evident sarcasm.

"It is."

"How's the safe house?"

"Unpleasant."

"I wasn't enquiring about the facilities. Simply whether it is compromised or not."

"No, it fine. I had no other difficulties." Konstantin wasn't lying, just believed his altercation with Dave the Rave had been an inconsequential incident.

"Good. I'll be in touch in the next twenty-four hours with an address."

"Local?"

"I doubt it. Too risky."

Konstantin didn't like the sound of that. Didn't say goodbye as Lamb departed.

Snubnose

Dave wished he was at a rave. Off his tits on some ecstasy. Drenched in sweat, dancing like a bastard. Be a hell of a lot happier than he was now.

Miserable. That's how he felt, on the biggest downer ever. Found the big man's abode but no call from Charlie. Assumed he'd been bullshitting him. So instead Dave kept watch on the entrance to the flats. Sat in a bus shelter. Didn't get any strange looks from passers-by. Plenty of crazies around here.

Checked his watch for the thousandth time. Another hour gone. Less than twenty four now until Frank wanted payment. Every movement of the second hand potentially a moment less of Dave's existence. If it was, what a way to spend his remaining time on earth.

Cursed himself for getting even further in debt with Frank. For calling him and buying a gun on credit. But he was on his own and needed an advantage over the big Russian.

He considered again sprinting the short distance to the station. Catching the first train that stopped. Going anywhere, as long as it was miles away from Frank.

But Dave knew it was pointless. He didn't have any money for a start. And that Frank would one day catch up with him. Make him pay with pain. No, the odds were better on finding this man. Sorting it out himself.

He just hoped it could be soon. Time was running out.

A Storm Is Coming

Konstantin was glad it was late in the day. Less glare to exacerbate his hangover.

Easy to work out where 'home' was. The apartment block rose high above everything else. He started to lope down the hill, back towards the amusement arcade, away from the police station. After a few minutes' walking he reached a pub. Seedy looking place that overlooked the harbour.

He stopped, considered walking in, discovered he was penniless. Spent it, or lost it. Wasn't sure which. Either way, couldn't afford a drink. But knew he had plenty more cash in the flat.

Got walking again. Realised there was someone at his side. Large backpack slung over his shoulder, strong odour, slight limp.

"Just wanted to give my thanks," said Ralph. "Very few show me real kindness."

Konstantin shrugged, said, "I not do anything."

"Kept me out of the halfway house. I like sleeping under the stars this time of year. But that Gregory, he's always there to move me along. Officious bastard."

"Where you tonight?"

"Don't know yet," said Ralph.

"Look like rain."

The Russian nodded towards a menacingly black cloud on the horizon.

"It does."

"There's room in the flat."

Closer To A Conclusion

Dave the Rave jolted when he saw the Russian. Couldn't mistake the man's bulk. He was with someone else. The tramp. Everyone knew him. In fact Dave had pissed on him once. The vagrant had been so drunk he hadn't even noticed. Which took all the fun out of it.

He pulled his hood further over his face, turned away slightly so his features fell into shadow. He was well practised at concealing himself from prying eyes, particularly electronic ones.

But there was no need. The guy didn't even glance in Dave's direction. Which just made him angrier. The arrogance of the man.

He fingered the gun. Felt the gnarled grip, cold to the touch, even though it had nestled in his jacket all day. It would only take a single bullet to put everything right, he was sure. Present a corpse to Frank, that had to be enough to prove he was destined for and capable of bigger things. Give him time to wipe the slate clean.

Only one more fact would make the situation perfect. Knowing when the Russian was going to leave. Then he'd be ready.

Last Night On Earth

"He ain't staying here," said Charlie, hand on the door. Like that was going to be any sort of barrier.

Konstantin pushed past the man, flattened him against the wall, stomach protruding. Ralph followed in his wake, nodded, said, "Better than the halfway house."

Charlie grimaced, slammed the door shut.

"You sleep here," Konstantin pointed to the box room he'd forced Charlie to inhabit. "Sofa," he said to Charlie, the question half formed on his lips.

"Not fucking fair."

"Life not fair," agreed Konstantin.

"Thanks," said Ralph, oblivious to Charlie's distress.

Konstantin entered his room. Flicked the light on. Knew immediately it had been searched. But only one item was worth stealing. Good, still there. And so was the concealed money. The knife had gone though. And the cash from the suitcase.

Went back into the living room, caught Charlie pulling his trousers down.

"Hey, little privacy here?" he shouted. Whatever he was going to say next was choked off as Konstantin folded his fingers around the man's throat.

"Want to know one thing," he said.

Charlie tried to nod, failed to do so as oxygen starvation was affecting his motor skills. Konstantin noted the change in colour of Charlie's skin, like his face was about to explode. Released the pressure, let the man sag back onto the sofa.

"What?" he croaked.

"Who went through bag?"

"Not me," he lied.

"Sure. Who else?"

"Just some guy. Never seen him before. Said he'd kill me if he didn't let me in."

Konstantin didn't believe the fiction. Described Dave briefly, got a nod from Charlie. Knew he'd have to leave the flat, but was desperate for a few hours of proper sleep. He hadn't been allowed to properly rest in the cell. Been checked on regularly by the cops and when he had shut his painful eyes it was a rest founded on alcohol and a hangover. Less than ideal.

So a few hours in bed, then he and Ralph would depart. No idea where to, but he'd worry about that tomorrow.

Left Charlie cowering on the sofa.

Promised himself he'd see his daughter one more time before he left forever.

A Red Or A Blue?

Charlie's throat was raw. He kept rubbing at the red marks on his skin. Looked like he had a rash, rather than nearly been choked to death.

It took him hours to build up the nerve to sneak past the big man's room, even though he heard snoring within minutes of him retiring. Thought it may be pretence, didn't want to take the risk. Couldn't afford to change a second pair of pants. He didn't have any more to slip into.

That and the guy Dave was still in the bus shelter. Could see his legs. Hadn't moved all day. Not for food or a piss.

Charlie took the stairs. Was petrified the distant sound of the lift mechanism would wake his unwelcome guest. That and the bloody thing kept breaking down intermittently. Now was not the time to get himself stuck in there. Most days he wouldn't have cared. Something to do at least.

There was no traffic on the road, no pedestrians on the pavement, not even shitehawks in the sky when Charlie exited. He ran across the thoroughfare to the bus shelter. Saw Dave jerk when he stepped inside. Was sure he caught a glimpse of gunmetal. Gulped. Made him want to be in the flat even more.

"He's here," said Charlie.

"I know, I saw them walk in. When will the Russian be leaving?"

Charlie shrugged, said, "Didn't tell me. But he's sleeping for the dead."

That brought a smile to Dave's face. Charlie shuddered.

"You need to give me a signal, let me know he's on his way down. So I can be ready."

"Okay." Charlie thought for a moment. Figured Dave wouldn't know exactly which window was his, there were so many, and the sun would glint off the glass when it rose over the horizon. Hard to see much.

"I've a Man United towel I'll hang off the balcony."

Dave spat. "Fuck's sake, man. I'll not move for those red bastards. Got one for Chelsea?"

Charlie shook his head. "It's all I have."

"Shite, when this is over I'll get you proper blue gear."

"Look, I've gotta get back."

"Right United it is. Keep your mouth shut that I agreed to this, though. If the boys ever find out I'll never hear the last of it."

Charlie didn't wait. Turned and dashed across the road. Back up the stairs. Much slower than he would have liked, but he was an unfit man. His chest ached by the time he reached his front door. Stood outside for a couple of minutes to let his heart rate and breathing slow. He was panting like a rapist.

Couldn't believe his luck when in the corridor. The big guy was sound asleep, snoring unabated. He crashed out on the sofa, dog tired but knew he had to stay conscious, so he stood up. Opened all the windows, turned the television on low and made coffee. In a vase.

Should be enough to keep him awake 'til morning.

Collision Course

Konstantin felt like his head had barely touched the pillow before he was waking again. Felt bone tired.

No rest for the eternally wicked, he thought.

Crashed out in his clothes. Not the first time.

Checked his watch. Would more than likely make it to the ground floor in time to see his daughter pass by if he shook a tail feather.

Found Charlie fast asleep on the sofa. Mouth open, line of dried drool bisected his chin. A vase, of all things, tipped over by his side. Brown stain on the carpet.

Konstantin grabbed the quick dribble that passed for a shower, got changed. Packed his bag, stuffed the money right at the bottom.

In the box room Ralph was awake. He was lying on his back, staring at the ceiling. He too had slept fully dressed, kept his boots on as well. The sheets were a mess. Konstantin mentally shrugged. Couldn't imagine being house-proud was high on Charlie's life list.

"Ready?" asked Konstantin.

"Always," replied Ralph. Swung his legs off the bed, picked up his rucksack.

On the way out, a childish thought struck Konstantin. He gave into it, slammed the door. Sounded like a gunshot. Hoped it woke the bastard.

Pressed the button for the lift. Waited. Checked his watch.

Glory, Glory Man United

Charlie jerked upright. Looked around blearily. Then realised – it was the morning! He bolted off the sofa like a fox with a hound on its arse. Ran down the corridor. Both rooms were empty. Shit!

He could hear the lift moving, the unmistakable clank and squeal of worn cogs.

The towel. He needed the towel. Couldn't grab it last night because it was in the room the big guy had been snoring in. He yanked open the cupboard door, pulled every last textile item out.

It wasn't there.

Then he remembered. The bloody thing was in a pile he hadn't yet sorted for washing. In the corner of the bathroom. Ran in. Threw all manner of clothing up in the air. Saw a flash of red. Grabbed it.

Belted into the living room, heaved open the egress onto the narrow balcony. Flapped the towel wildly.

Slipped out of his grip…

Dave the Rave was in another world, half dead with fatigue, when he heard the car crash, metal grinding onto metal. Moments later, swearing as one driver blamed the other. Narrowed his eyes when he saw a red towel over the windscreen of the vehicle in front. Would have totally obscured his view.

He scanned upwards. Caught sight of a figure on a balcony waving frantically.

Dave leapt up, hand on the gun inside his jacket. Grinned.

Fucking Man United. Might just save his life yet.

The Hammer Drops

For once the lift arrived quickly. Only had to descend a floor or two. The doors stuck two-thirds open, as usual. The pair squeezed in. Konstantin pressed the button. The letter 'G' almost worn away. Slow descent.

Stepped out, across the hallway and outside. Konstantin looked left and right, hoping to catch a glimpse of the girl, but instead heard the unmistakable snick of a hammer being cocked. And not the type used to hit nails.

"Got you, you bastard," said someone.

Konstantin swivelled slowly. Ignored the huge barrel that would eject a projectile at sub-sonic velocity capable of killing him at many yards, never mind less than a hair's breadth.

He recognised the man. His first interaction in Margate two days ago that had led to this.

A death.

Konstantin realised he didn't care. Dropped his bag. Leant forward slightly, felt the gun press to his forehead, enjoyed the cold kiss of metal shaped to kill.

"Go on, do it," said Konstantin. "I tired. End me."

Dave the Rave laughed. Said, "Whatever you want man. It's one or the other of us anyway."

Konstantin darkened his vision. Felt the happiest he had been for… he couldn't remember. His one regret – not seeing her again. But in a few seconds he wouldn't be able to care any more.

Then he heard Dave grunt. An expulsion of air, decorated with pain. Snapped his eyes open, saw Ralph struggling with him, forcing the gun down.

BANG!

Ralph stiffened, mouth open in an O as big as the weapon's barrel. The tramp stepped back, blood on his hands. Dave dropped the gun to the floor. Turned. Ran like he had the devil at his heels.

Konstantin caught Ralph, lowered him gently to the ground before he collapsed. Placed the tramp's head in his lap.

Pressed both hands on the wound. Felt the blood pulse through his fingers.

"Give me something to staunch wound!" shouted Konstantin.

No one moved.

"Quickly! He die otherwise."

Somebody bent down, passed Konstantin a black jacket. Shiny material. He applied it to the gaping hole, but it was unsuitable.

"Grab my bag. Coat inside, pull out."

The girl did as she was told. Rooted around, found the heavy, green-ish coat, lined with fleece. Pressed it down, tried to ignore the tramp's groan of pain. As she did so the grey lining quickly turned red.

Ralph lifted a shaky hand, placed it on Konstantin's. The grip was weak.

"Time for me to go, I'm afraid," he whispered.

"I sorry."

"No. No. It wasn't your fault. All mine. Thank you."

Konstantin opened his mouth to speak, but Ralph's eyes were blank.

The Russian gritted his teeth. Needed to scream, but instead looked up, wanted to know who'd helped a tramp in his last moments and an outcast.

Gazed into the face of his daughter.

The pair sat together in the back of an ambulance, neither speaking. The world was in turmoil around them, yet in their little bubble, all remained calm and at peace.

Eventually Konstantin said, "Thank you."

She shrugged, "I couldn't stand by and watch a man die." Like others had.

More silence. Then she said, "Do I know you?"

Konstantin turned to her, said the hardest word, "No."

Voices outside broke the spell.

"Excuse me." Constable Gregory stood in the entrance to the ambulance. Looked sheepish, yet determined. Seemed he'd finally stopped crying for the tramp. He nodded to the girl. "Your mother is here."

She slid out from under the blanket. Touched the back of Konstantin's hand as she stood. His skin felt like it was on fire.

Gregory took the girl's place.

"The Super wants you to be kept for questioning," said Gregory.

Konstantin shrugged.

"I've sent my colleague away for a cup of tea. This is your chance to clear off."

The Russian couldn't quite believe what Gregory was saying.

"Why?"

"Ralph was my friend. You were there at the end for him."

"I try not to hit you too hard."

The constable was halfway to verbalising a response when Konstantin punched him. Gregory folded onto the bench.

Konstantin waited a moment, then clambered out. Saw the girl with her mother, blonde hair pulled back into a ponytail as ever. They were in an embrace, tears in the mother's eyes. At last she pulled away.

"You could have been killed!" she said.

"But I wasn't and I had to help the poor old man."

The pair hugged again. The mother's eyes flicked to the ambulance. Saw Konstantin standing there.

Smiled.

Konstantin walked away. Couldn't look back.

Dave Raves No More

Two Weeks Later

Dave the Rave walked the streets of Manchester, looking for a job. So far, no joy. Trouble was he needed an interpreter from Northern to Southern – couldn't understand a word that was being said to him.

He had no idea why he'd picked this place. Supposed it seemed far enough away from Margate. Certainly felt like a different country, that was for sure. Dave wondered when Man United would be playing Chelsea, decided he'd try and blag a ticket. For good luck.

After another couple of fruitless hours, Dave wandered back home. If that's what it could be called. A shabby one bedroom bedsit on a shitty council estate with a worse view. Knew he had to get work soon, otherwise he wouldn't be able to afford even this place. The dole was barely covering the costs.

On the third floor Dave pushed at his door, it was slightly ajar. He couldn't believe he'd been robbed already. There was nothing worth nicking, only possessed what he'd frantically stuffed in a bag immediately after the tramp got it.

The door swung back.

"What a dump, Dave," said Frank McGavin. "I don't even want to sit down it's that bad. Who knows what I'll catch? Mind you, you're here."

"How did you find me?"

"Bit of a mistake signing on, Dave. Red rag to a pissed off bull your name is. Amazing what a few quid greasing the right palms can provide."

Dave turned on his heel, but his one skill failed him for the last time. A man mountain blocked his path.

"There'll be no getting past Dirty Harry," said Frank. "So we can either do this the easy way or the hard way."

Dave slumped, felt a huge hand clamp down on a shoulder, heard Frank say, "Good boy."

Two days later, a man's body was found floating in the Manchester Ship Canal, the face unrecognisable. Almost every bone had been broken. He'd been literally beaten to death.

Donning The Cowl

Three Months Later

It had been a busy time since Ralph's death. Konstantin needed something to help him forget.

Within a day he'd discovered a dilapidated row of terraced houses on the brink of demolition, bought them for a song. Claimed to be a developer. The estate agent didn't care. Only the money was important.

He'd moved in immediately, picked the residence just off centre. Started doing it up. Got all the supplies early or late in the day. When there were fewer people around. Liked the fact the house had bars on the windows already. Liked even more that there was a small cellar dug into soft chalk. That would be expanding soon.

Today. Decided it was time. The beard was matted enough. Covered most of his face. His hair, too, was significantly longer. Donned the crappy clothes he'd bought from charity shops. Fingerless gloves, even though it was the warm end of a summer it would still be chilly, standing around all day.

Finally, he shrugged on the green-ish coat. He'd carefully washed out as much of the blood from the lining as possible, but left the outside untouched. The coat was heavy, reassuring. The best friend he had now.

On the walk to his new post, Konstantin stopped at a phone box. Dialled the number from a piece of paper. Waited for the connection. The tone was a single purr. Somewhere abroad.

"Yes?" said Mr. Lamb.

"I just want let you know I've moved on."

"That's good. Thank you for informing me."

Konstantin ended the call. Crumpled up the paper, knew he wouldn't need Lamb and they'd never meet again. He had people to protect.

This was his place. In front of a small row of terraced houses, Buenos Ayres Back to the sea, he watched the train station and its passengers.

Three hours later she came. No longer wore the school uniform. Met a friend, they hugged, kissed like women do.
Konstantin went utterly unnoticed.
He liked that.

Plastic
Fantastic

The Scream

Konstantin walked. Heard a shriek nearby, but immediately tuned it out. Like white noise. There, but not. It was normal behaviour – Saturday, late at night, after all.

This one, high pitched then tapered with a laugh, emanated from a drunk. Of course it was a woman, always seemed to be the female of the species these days that got the most hammered, caused the most bother. Directly or indirectly.

He passed a chippy. Glanced in and saw the hammered offender playing up. Staff well behind the counter. Patrons pressed around the wall. She suddenly lost it. Flipped. Threw the bag of deep fried potato at a rival, followed by her flailing self. Hair was yanked and a few punches thrown.

Konstantin didn't break stride. Not for him to intervene. Not his town. Not his people. Not his problem.

The Scots have a multitude of names for rain, same for the Eskimos (or was it Inuit now?) and snow, it's surprising how many different types of scream there were:

Joy, of a child playing in the cold sea. Most often heard in the summer, drifted on the breeze to him.

Pleasure, of sex, an orgasm. Something the Russian hadn't experienced for a long time.

Loss, of someone or something close to you. All too familiar.

Pain, of torture or a beating. That Konstantin was most acquainted with. Still literally bore the scars.

The list went on.

He paced a back road, avoiding the main drag despite the locals having learned to leave him alone. Until Konstantin, tramps had been seen as an easy target. Wasted wasters. To be pissed on or beaten up. But not this one. After he'd kicked the shit out of a third group of lads, word got around and stayed there.

The altercations were seemingly never reported, well Konstantin hadn't had any trouble with the police. Couldn't imagine some puffed up hoodie confessing to getting slapped around by a badly dressed bearded man in a green-ish coat who smelt like he had more alcohol than blood in his veins, but could move with astonishingly co-ordinated speed and ferocity.

Konstantin reached the place he couldn't call home. Entered the seemingly derelict row of terraced houses by a rear entrance. Newly installed security gates kept the undesirables out. Didn't want any prying eyes. Too many secrets to preserve. Once inside, he discarded his clothing, walked around in underwear and T-shirt. Kept the heating on all the time, wanted to be warm. Spent too much time outside, cold. No bills to pay either, another problem for someone else.

His residence appeared standard enough. Sparsely furnished upstairs and down. But the normality ended there. Entrances cut through to the other houses – hidden transition routes to places with other purposes. The process of digging tunnels from the cellar through the soft chalk wasn't yet finished.

Entered a small gym, pulled on some well-used gloves, started pounding a punch bag that hung from the ceiling, moved as it swung, hit it low and hard. Worked up a torrential sweat, tried to drive out the frustration. The feeling of loss. Of being cut away. Like an appendix. Useless. Spare.

Totally failed.

Knock, Knock

There was a hammering. Literally. The repetitive rap reached Konstantin in his bedroom on the first floor. He awoke instantly, sat up, listened. Slid off the mattress, padded downstairs to the source. His front door. As he descended, the noise stopped. Stood in the hallway a moment. The same noise resumed yards away.

Konstantin wanted to see what was happening without having to step outside. Decided CCTV would be a good idea and resolved to install that next. Left it five minutes, pulled the door open, oblivious to his partial state of undress. Pyjama bottoms, nothing else. The early morning air was cool. Drone of distant traffic. Squawk of seagulls. Bastards.

There was a notice pinned to his door. Tore it down and read it. The terse words told him the terrace of houses must be refurbished or face a compulsory purchase, followed by demolition.

"Interfering bastards," said a voice. Easy, young, soft.

Konstantin looked up from the paper, saw a young woman. Raven haired. No make-up. Looked tired and drawn, like she'd had a late night. Hair roughly tied up. Short dressing gown showing a lot of leg, tied tight at the waist. She regarded him, eyebrow cocked in a permanently amused fashion. Eyes flickered from scar to scar on the Russian's torso.

"Excuse me?" Konstantin said. Accent dropped, indeterminate English inflection applied.

"I said, they're interfering bastards, the council. Can't keep their fucking noses out of what isn't their business."

She walked over, snatched the document from between his fingers, glanced over it. Snorted, said, "Same as mine." Passed it back. "Probably want to build some high density housing. Cram in a few more foreigners that haven't got jobs and can cream it off the state."

She paused, waited for Konstantin to fill in the gap. When he didn't, she said, "What do you think?"

"I've no idea."

She shrugged, like it didn't matter what they thought. That shit would happen regardless.

"I'm Fidelity by the way. We're neighbours. What's your name?" she said, pushed a hand out, took his, shook, then released. Arm dropped back to his side, like the muscles were atrophied. She paused a moment, stretched out again in an effort to touch one of his blemishes.

Konstantin grabbed her wrist, said, "I'm nobody." Torpor finally shaken off, wits about him again. "Just a guy."

Fidelity smiled. "That's okay love, I understand. No one reveals their true self in my game either. Now, would you mind letting go of me?"

Konstantin slowly released his grip. Went back inside without saying another word. Left Fidelity standing there. Half smile still on her upturned lips.

Konstantin took a slug of coffee, looked over the document again. It was trouble.

Then he heard a noise. The smash of glass. He sighed. Tensed his jaw. Heard a laugh. Blew air through his nostrils. Knew he shouldn't react, but couldn't help it. Pushed himself upright. Rolled his neck, heard the crack of a couple of tendons.

In moments he was outside, in the alley that ran along the back of his house. Full of junk. The same kids were there. Messing around, making problems for the neighbours. Konstantin walked up to them. Four teenagers turned to face him. All nearing six feet. Spindly. Full of nervous energy and pussy spots.

"What you want?" the leader demanded. Shock of hair covering his eyes. Hoodie pulled up. Permanent slouch, fixed scowl. Already inured to life. The other three similarly dressed. Not quite as tall, but looked like they hadn't been eating enough.

"We've discussed this before," Konstantin replied.

"You what, mate? Discussed? What are you talking about, old man?"

The others snickered. A few nudges passed around.

"We agreed you wouldn't come around here again." Kept the tone level, reasonable.

"Nah, mate. You suggested it. I didn't agree. We've the right to go wherever I want."

Konstantin sighed. Could see this was only going to go one way. Wasn't in the mood to step down.

"Last warning," he said. "I couldn't care less what you get up to. As long as it's not around here."

"Whatever, man. I'm bored of this shit. Now fuck off."

More laughing. The leader turned back to his friends. Lit a joint. The sweet smoke filled the air. Reminded Konstantin of days in Amsterdam. In the back street coffee houses.

The Russian began to count to ten. Reached two, which was a record. Kicked out. Hit the leader in the back of the knee. Ignored the shriek of pain. Punched him hard in the right kidney, forearm to the back of the head.

Waited for the others to come to him. Bounced lightly on the balls of his feet, fists up. Made a nice change to be hitting flesh that reacted, instead of a passive bag which simply took it. Half of him hoped they'd back off, the other half that they'd be stupid.

They were worse than stupid, pulled knives. Like that was going to freak out Konstantin. He grinned. The trio paused a moment until the leader, still down on the ground, yelled, "Get him!"

He was, literally, fighting fit. Months of training and a pent-up anger lent Konstantin speed and power. The first one came in swinging, head on. The whistle of the knife was surprisingly loud, like everyone was holding their breath and it was the only noise in the world. Konstantin leaned back, let the blade swish past his chest, planted a massive fist into the kid's jaw. Heard it crack. The kid's head snapped backwards and he was down.

Konstantin immediately kicked out with his right leg, caught the second kid rushing at him from the side. A hard foot straight into the bollocks, vicious uppercut as the kid folded over. His eyes went glassy. Three down in as many seconds.

The last kid stared at the devastation Konstantin had caused. Lifted his eyes to meet the Russian's. Must have seen the fury within because he took a couple of steps back, dropped his weapon, turned and ran.

Konstantin blew out a huge breath, dropped his fists. Bent down and scooped up all the knives. He'd destroy them later. Crossed over to the leader, squatted down next to him. He cringed, more so when Konstantin smiled. He said, "Are we clear now?"

The leader nodded vigorously.

"Good boy. If I ever see you here again, I'll get *really* nasty. Understood?"

More vigorous head movement.

Konstantin stood. Felt eyes on him. Looked upwards, saw a figure sitting on a windowsill, cigarette between slim fingers. Must have seen everything. Fidelity winked. Drew the curtains, shut him off.

He turned on the shower, turned the heat up, got it scalding. Stepped in. Felt the spray hit his skin like shards of glass. Made him feel alive for a moment.

It had been months, but Konstantin still wasn't used to his new name. And the fact that he only had one. In the past he'd used many. Each day could be different. Often was. New place, new identity. Used until discarded.

Not any more. Now he was one person. Without a structure around him to tell him what to do. Where to go. What to infiltrate. Who to murder. And it was killing him. Konstantin turned in the water, let the jet beat down on his back, head bowed.

Began to thump the tiles with his palm.

Broke one.

Taser Time

The kid leant on the doorbell then on the wall. Felt like shit. Ached all over. Would be pissing blood for days, he knew.

Rang again, finally heard footsteps, shadow at the peephole.

"Open up, for fuck's sake!" he shouted. "It's me." Heard the lock twist.

"What do you want?" she asked, innocent look on her face and a smouldering fag in her lips.

"You owe us more money, lady."

"And why would that be?"

"You didn't say anything about getting a good shoeing from the guy."

"You're right, but I can't plan for every eventuality," she lied. "Anyway, why is it my problem?"

"Because we got a good shoeing, lady."

She shrugged. "You got paid didn't you?"

"Yeah, but not enough."

"Tough luck. A deal is a deal. A lesson for you to learn."

The kid started to get angry. Didn't like adults telling him what to do. Took it up a notch. "I don't like the way you're talking to me, bitch."

She shrugged again, said, "And that matters to me, why?"

He grinned, grabbed his crotch. "I'll show you why."

"A skinny shit like you, with such a tiny cock? I don't think so."

The kid's bellow of rage turned into one of pain as she rammed the Taser into his side, pressed the trigger, let 30,000 volts course through his body. For the second time in five minutes he hit the floor. Shook uncontrollably.

She bent down, whispered in his ear, "If you bring your spotty face to my door again I'll have my friend Nikos cut your balls off and shove them down your throat."

He looked at her with wide eyes.

"So you're aware who Nikos is?"

Blank stare, still shaking with the jolt.

"Because if you fuck with me, you fuck with him."

The kid couldn't do a response.

"Our deal is concluded," she said, then zapped him again. Went inside, closed the door.

She leant against the wall, blew out a big ball of tension. She'd got away with it. Nikos didn't want to protect her. Just the opposite. Thankfully, the kid was too stupid to realise.

Fidelity knew she was walking a tightrope with a long drop either side of her. Just hoped the big man from across the road would be there to catch her if she fell.

It took about fifteen minutes before the kid could talk. His first mumble was, "Who the fuck is Nikos?"

Strap It On

Konstantin sat at his PC. Pushed wet hair out of his eyes. A quick sweep of the internet showed Fidelity's assertion was, in fact, correct. He went onto the local newspaper's website. Didn't take long to find the article he wanted. A few weeks old already. Had been headline news.

Photo of some fat guy, shirt buttons bursting. Tie that looked like it was strangling him, face dark. High blood pressure. Be dead in a few years unless he lost a lot of weight and soon. Fatty had a name – Councillor Spray. Minor elected official. Small fish, small pond. Been in local politics for years. Spearheading a campaign to tear down derelict properties with absent landlords. If the owners failed to comply, the council did it for them. But Konstantin's houses only appeared dilapidated. Inside they were pristine.

A bit more searching revealed Spray was also taking credit for a recent campaign to drive out slum landlords. Illegal immigrants stuffed into small rooms. Photos of cops raiding houses. Arresting foreigners. Clearing out the problem.

The local superhero. Bet his pants had skid marks though. Laudable, but fighting a losing battle. But that wasn't the point. Scoring them was. This was politics after all.

Konstantin decided he had to know more about his enemy. Wondered how. The man moved in totally different circles and he was relatively new in town.

He heard a knocking at his door. Unusual and new. Konstantin opened the door. It felt like shaking hands with your left, rather than right. Not quite correct. Familiar, yet not.

It was Fidelity. She said, "Some good moves there."

Konstantin didn't reply. Unsure what to say. Fidelity looked at him, head tilted, amused smile on her features. Didn't wait to be asked, just walked inside uninvited. Left Konstantin at the entrance, hand on the knob. He closed it, words still trapped inside.

Fidelity had a quick glance around, popped her head into each room. Finally entered the kitchen. Dropped a large leather bag from her shoulder onto the floor. Leant against the counter, said, "Nice place you have."

"Thanks."

"Coffee would be nice."

Konstantin pulled a container of grounds down, began the ritual.

"Do you mind if I smoke?" she asked.

"Yes."

Fidelity placed a cigarette between bright red lips. Sparked up. Blew a stream of smoke upwards in a clear challenge. Raised an eyebrow at him.

Konstantin took her in. Quite different to earlier. A lot more make-up on. Bare legs beneath a rain coat. Flat shoes. Hair pulled up into a high style atop her skull. More alert expression on her doll's face, like she'd finally got some sleep.

Looked good. Felt bad.

"You didn't tell me your name yesterday," she said, slight hint of admonishment in her voice.

"Paul," he lied as he filled a kettle with water. Put it on the stove to boil.

"Hmm, you don't look much like a Paul to me."

Konstantin shrugged. Wasn't quite sure why he'd supplied Fidelity with an alternate moniker. Something about her that made his hackles rise. Probably the danger in her eyes. He liked it.

Hint of a playful smile, she said, "Anyway *Paul,* I wanted to talk to you."

"Well, here we are," he said, leant against the counter. "Talk away."

"It's about our little shared problem."

Blank expression.

She sighed, said, "The compulsory purchase notice?"

"Oh. Yes. I forgot. Lot on at the moment."

"Wow, you must lead an amazing life if having your house repossessed is a low priority."

He didn't know what to say. Was a bit shocked he kept losing the use of his tongue when in this woman's presence.

Fortunately the kettle started to bubble away, giving Konstantin the opportunity to break eye and mental contact.

A minute later he handed Fidelity a steaming mug. She swapped it for a dead cigarette butt which he binned.

"Look, I'd better be honest with you," Fidelity said. It was Konstantin's turn to arch an eyebrow. "I have an unusual day job. Well, night job really."

"Oh?"

She sighed, said, "Perhaps it's best just to show you."

Fidelity peeled off her coat. She wore a leather corset underneath. Laced tightly, it pushed impressive breasts skyward. She bent down, opened up her bag. Pulled out a strap-on. A rather large beast.

"I'm a dominatrix. Men pay me to give them a hard time. Literally. My working name is Plastic Fantastic."

"And what, you think I should become a new customer?"

Fidelity laughed. "No! You're clearly not the type. I think you prefer to give the orders, rather than take them. It's one of my clients you may be interested in. Councillor Richard Spray."

Konstantin shrugged, kept his expression neutral. "What's your proposal?"

Fidelity shook her head, said, "You're not exactly a barrel of laughs, are you?"

The Russian said nothing, elicited a sigh from the dominatrix. She shrugged her coat back on.

"Okay, the man is in love with me. Says he'll leave his wife. I've told him countless times that I'm not interested. I don't want to be in a relationship with anyone again. Ever."

"Go on."

"If I ask, Richard will revoke the purchase order on your house, but first I need something in exchange."

"I'm not surprised."

"I owe someone money. A guy called Nikos."

"Loan shark?"

"Yes."

"Stupid."

Fidelity went as red as her lipstick. "You know nothing about me."

Konstantin eyed the plastic appendage that was still on view, said, "Actually I know too much about you."

"So you won't help me?"

"No. I don't want to get involved. I don't do that any more."

"What about your house?"

"I'll fix that myself, thanks."

"Well, fuck you," Fidelity spat. Dropped her cup on the floor. It shattered. Sprayed ceramic shards and coffee everywhere. She grabbed her bag. Stormed out of the kitchen.

Five seconds later the door slammed. Sounded like a gunshot. Konstantin shrugged. Went to get a dustpan and brush.

Women.

No Pimp Zone

Fidelity stamped along the street. She was receiving some odd looks, but couldn't care less. Her coat flapped open, strap-on still in her hand. Eventually shoved it into her bag.

She was furious. And panicking. Wondered whether she should have told the pretend Paul more. Knew she should have. Given him more of a sob story. But next to impossible for her. Fidelity had to be in control, the need was spliced into her genes. Made her what she was. And she always got what she wanted. Until now.

Her head whirled. The possibilities open to her had dwindled. From one to zero. What was she going to do now? Fidelity had no idea. Perhaps Richard would. She'd be with him in fifteen minutes. Lengthened her stride.

The man followed Fidelity at an easy pace. Knew where she was going. Swarthy. Sunglasses. Slicked back hair. Casual clothes, but cast iron resolve. He lit a fag. Enjoyed the walk.

Fidelity entered the hotel, swept past reception without being challenged. They knew her. A good customer. As was Richard. She stepped into the lift. One of the old fashioned types. Where you had to close a grille gate yourself. Vintage death trap. Pressed the button for the third floor. Steadied herself as the cage jerked. Changed from her flat shoes into high boots.

The lift halted. Fidelity reversed the process, exited into the corridor. Found the room she wanted. Knocked. Door was opened almost immediately. Like he'd been waiting. Which he had.

"How did it go?" Spray asked, concern stitched across his flabby jaw.

Fidelity entered the room. Large double bed, drawer unit and flat screen TV the only other furniture. Pushed a smile onto her face, let her coat fall to the floor in the narrow entranceway. Revealed the corset. Heard Spray gasp.

"Later, darling. Play time first."

Spray didn't need telling twice. Trampled the expensive material in his rush to grab her.

"Slow down big boy," she chided, put a palm on his chest to halt his advance. "Let me get prepared first." Fidelity dropped a hand to her bag for the sex toy, but before she could undo the clasp, came a knock at the door.

"For God's sake, who's that!" said Richard, trousers round his ankles. Loose change from his pockets scattered like confetti.

"Room service!" heard faintly through the wood. "Champagne on the house."

Fidelity said, "Nothing to do with me." Shrugged. "But if it's free…"

He sighed, pulled up his trousers, fastened the button, left the zip down. Returned to the door. Opened up. Staggered back as it was immediately shoved inwards, hard.

A man entered, two more at his shoulder. He smiled. Bad teeth, crooked and misshapen. He said, "How fortune smiles on me. My two least favourite birds with one stone!"

Fidelity said, "Oh my God. Nikos." Put a hand to her mouth. Closed her eyes. Like that would make him go away.

"Like that's going to make me go away," Nikos laughed.

"What do you want?" Richard demanded. Got ignored while Nikos stared at Fidelity. "Do you know who I am?"

"Shut the fuck up, man," Nikos said, backhanded the Councillor. The slap was loud, rocked Richard. Fell to his knees. Blood trickled from his nose onto the floor.

Nikos nodded at his men. Big bastards. Lots of old tattoos on bunched muscles. They picked Richard up, dragged him to the bed. Threw him down. Was like moving a sack of spuds. Soft, yet lumpy.

"To answer your question, yes I know who you are. Councillor Spray, the man ready to sweep away the dross that blights this fair town. I think that's how you put it?"

Richard half nodded.

Nikos took off his sunglasses, folded them, said, "Well I'm the dross you refer to."

Spray paled.

Nikos crossed the short distance to Fidelity. Circumnavigated her, a few inches distant. Looked her over, like he was evaluating an animal at an auction.

"Looking good Fi," he said. "Looking mighty good."

"Thank you," she replied. Tried to force some resolve into her voice. Would not let any man overpower her. Could not.

"Have you got my money?"

"You know I don't."

Nikos sucked in his breath. "I wasn't quite sure which I preferred. A healthy financial profit or owning you. Now decision time is here? Definitely the latter."

"Fidelity, do you owe this man a debt?"

"Stay out of this Richard."

"I can't, I'm already involved."

"Oh dear Fi, another man sucked into your little schemes? Tut, tut." Nikos shook his head. Looked at Spray with affected pity. "You're a fool, man."

"I'll pay you whatever she owes. Plus 10%"

"He is generous this one!" Nikos said. "Care to make an increased bid for the whore's heart?"

"20%!"

"Richard, don't," Fidelity said. "You're just making it worse."

"It doesn't matter, I only want to get you out of this."

Nikos shook his head. "It's too late, Richard. I've already decided I'm going to allow Fidelity to repay her debt over the long term. Bit by bit."

"I don't understand," Richard said.

"I won't let you pimp me," Fidelity whispered, undid the clasp.

"You don't have a choice," Nikos laughed.

Fidelity let her bag fall, swung the strap-on at the loan shark's head.

Hospital Pass

Konstantin hadn't slept well. The girl, on his mind. Not sure whether it was a dream or a nightmare. Whatever, it was unsettling.

Knock at the door. The Russian shook his head. Resolved to get better at keeping people away. Maybe get a dog. Turned into banging, the side of a fist. Wouldn't stop.

Konstantin yanked open the door, shouted, "What?"

"Fuck's sake, just got a message for you," said the kid, took a step back. It was the one Konstantin had folded yesterday with the kidney punch. The leader.

"I told you not to come back."

The kid shrugged, said, "Fidelity told me to and what she says, I do. Thought about saying no, though. Mad bitch tasered me. You don't know what she's like…"

Konstantin stopped the dirge mid-flow. Shut the door. Couldn't quite close it though as the kid rammed a foot in the way. Squealed like a girl when it was crushed.

"Fucking hell, mate! Just give me ten seconds and I'll go. Promise."

"You've got five."

The kid nearly made it.

Konstantin climbed off the bus. Resolved to get himself some wheels as well as a dog. But not at the same time. Would look odd.

Asked at reception where to go. By pure chance it was visiting time. Not that that would have stopped him.

Entered the ward. Eight beds, four against each wall, walkway between. Most had curtains drawn, whispered voices behind. Only one silent. Parted the brittle material. Saw a fat man in bed, badly beaten. Face bandaged. Leg and arm in a cast. Been made a mess of. Would need a shitload of painkillers.

Stepped out again, bumped into Fidelity. Spilt the drink she was carrying.

"You took your time," she said.

"Public transport," Konstantin shrugged.

The pair sat opposite sides of a small table in the canteen. Fidelity had dumped the plastic cup of watery tea. Gained a mug of steaming coffee. So had the Russian. It tasted dreadful.

"I need something stronger in this," she said.

"Who's the guy?"

Fidelity shrugged. "Just a guy. A client. Wrong place, wrong time."

"What happened?" Konstantin asked.

"Why do you care?"

"I'm trying to work out whether I do or not."

"You're a strange man."

"You're hardly a model citizen yourself."

She laughed, a short, sharp stab at levity. Didn't work.

"What happened?" Konstantin repeated.

"Nikos happened."

"Start at the beginning."

"When you tell me your real name."

Sighed, said, "Konstantin." Elicited a small smile of triumph.

"Now tell me yours."

Another smile. "It really is Fidelity."

"So talk," he said.

She did. About the loan, had expenses. Hated taking anything from a man, but sometimes you have no choice in life. The debt had ramped up, Nikos accelerating the interest. Because he wanted her for himself. But she couldn't have that. Couldn't be owned again. She'd seen Konstantin, big guy, no fear, and thought he'd help.

"I was wrong," Fidelity said.

"It happens."

"Not to me."

She picked up the coffee, winced.

"They hurt you?"

Nodded, said, "Yes, just to make sure I got the message this time. But not my face though. Left my best asset alone. Nikos isn't stupid."

"And the guy?" Konstantin was bothered by him.

66

"Look I've already told you. He got in the way. Another example."

The Russian sat back. Looked at the girl. Knew she was hiding something, but couldn't decide if it mattered.

"What's next?" he asked.

"I honestly don't know," she replied. "I can't see a way out. He could bury me and no one would ever know, no one would miss me."

"Maybe I would."

"You said it yourself. You don't get involved any more."

Konstantin shook his head. Knew this was bound to turn out badly, but said anyway, "Sometimes things change."

Scooter Boy

"You need some wheels," Fidelity said. "This is ridiculous."

"I've never required any until now. Anyway, I don't like records, vehicles have to be registered."

It was raining. Konstantin ignored the water running down his neck. Kept his eyes on the house.

"If you had a car we'd be dry. Not getting soaked to the skin."

"You insisted on coming along," he reminded her. "You could have left it all to me."

"Can't trust a man to do anything right."

"Is this your part-time occupation?"

"What?"

"Complaining."

"You're an arsehole, do you know that?"

Konstantin grinned.

After a couple of minute's peace, punctuated by a single clap of thunder, Fidelity broke the silence, said, "So... this is it?"

"For now. We just watch. Get to know the guy."

"Oh, I know him."

"Not in the right way."

Half an hour later Nikos exited, sporting wide sunglasses despite the weather. The two heavies either side of him. They negotiated the small flight of steps. Got into a car at the kerb. A Bentley. Black, shiny. Expensive. One of the heavies drove.

"Come on," Konstantin said. Put the camera away. He'd got some decent shots.

Fidelity sighed. Got on the back of the moped. Said, "Next time, can you steal something with a bit more style?"

"Promise," Konstantin said, gunned the hairdryer engine.

The pair tracked Nikos and his men for the rest of the day. Saw him cruise around town, heavies knocking on doors, demanding cash. They paused for lunch at a decent restaurant. The rain stopped about then. Fidelity's complaining didn't.

She bought them a sandwich from a nearby store while Konstantin maintained his vigil.

"Egg and cress?" he said.

"All they had," she shrugged, kept her expression impassive. Bit into something that looked far more palatable. "How much longer are we going to do this for?"

"As long as it takes."

"Great. I'm with Mr. Macho."

"I can take you home if you wish."

"Just so you understand, I'm not ducking out."

"I believe you."

She sighed, said, "Do you have to be so sarcastic?"

"Always."

Konstantin dropped Fidelity off fifteen minutes later. Said he'd see her later. Evening jaunt to the bars.

"What's your mobile number?" she asked.

"Don't have one," Konstantin replied.

"So how am I supposed to get in touch with you if things go wrong?" Incredulity in her tone.

He shrugged, said, "Don't get into trouble."

The bedraggled dominatrix waved as she entered her house. Shut the door. Told Konstantin she needed a shower. The Russian would do the same.

But first he had to get rid of the moped. It would than likely be reported stolen by now. He ambled for five minutes. Dumped it on a street corner. In full view.

Started to walk home, knew the moped would be gone very soon. Began to rain. Sighed.

Psycho

Fidelity felt miserable. Not because she was cold and wet, but from having to be economic with the truth. Again. She couldn't help it, was basically conditioned to keep her thoughts inside, but it still felt wrong. The guy was just trying to help her. He seemed genuine. Which puzzled her.

She climbed into the shower, the temperature turned right up. She looked at the bruise just under her rib cage. Where she'd caught the banister as she ran. Fidelity hadn't quite told Konstantin all. Neither the loan shark or his men had hit her, they hadn't had chance.

When Fidelity had swung the strap-on at Nikos it'd bought her a few precious seconds. Enough to get out the room, slamming the door shut behind her. Down the stairs, hitting the bannister, all three flights, pursued by the heavies. Not easy in high boots. Into the lobby, slowed to a walk, nodded at the concierge. Straight out the entrance and grabbed a waiting cab. First bit of luck she'd had all day. By the time the heavies were on the pavement, she was gone.

Fidelity spent twenty minutes under the pulsating jets until the hot water ran out. She shrieked as a blast of cold hit her. Some frantic twisting of the tap and the stream died away. She felt around for the towel she'd left just beyond the curtain, water still in her eyes. The cloth touched her fingertips. She wiped her face, wrapped it around her body. Stopped short.

She hadn't left the towel there, it had been on a chair at the top of the bath, not suspended in mid-air. Tentatively she drew the curtain back, saw Nikos. Not grinning for once. Black eye and red welt across the left side of his face.

"Hello, bitch," he said. "Nowhere for you to run this time." Pointed at a heavy in the doorway. Bared his bad teeth.

Hunting Nikos

Banged on her door. No answer. Repeated the tattoo. Stepped back into the street, looked up at the windows. No lights on. Went round the back into the alley. Stared up at her window. Found the same absence of illumination. Curtains closed.

Konstantin considered throwing stones at her window. Dismissed it as a stupid idea half a second later. For two reasons – she was tough and a woman. If he woke her he'd be in trouble.

He turned his jacket collar up, started the walk into town.

Hit the first bar, even though it was early. Konstantin hadn't wanted to hang around at home. Things to do, Nikos to find. There were a few people out, hammered already. Probably had been all day. Just topping themselves up. Loud blare of music. Flashing lights.

Took enough time to work out who to talk to. Began to show the photos of Nikos. No one knew him. Even when cash inducements offered. Very puzzling. But, as always, the solution eventually resulted. Effort equals reward.

Konstantin was in a club. Beer in front of him, first of the night. Seated with back against a wall. Eyes everywhere. Ignored the writhing bodies. Watched for those standing still. Saw someone. Fixed stare. Eyes on him.

The man began to cross the dance floor, ably avoided the bouncing bodies, waving arms. Konstantin stood as he neared the table, didn't want to be in the weaker position if push literally came to shove.

He was short, wiry, nervous twitch on him. Said, "Hear you've been asking about Nikos."

Konstantin nodded. Kept his hands loose and down by his sides. Everyone else around him had metaphorically gone. Only this guy mattered now.

"You're to come with me," he said,

Konstantin didn't move, said, "Where?"

"Two choices. Out the back and you find out what you want, or out the front and never return."

The Russian mentally shrugged, began to follow. Didn't need to cut around the dancers this time, hit a fire exit a few yards away. No alarms sounded when Shorty pushed at it. He held the door open, waved Konstantin through. Heard it slam behind him.

He found himself in a dark alley. Eyes didn't take long to adjust, been dim in the club anyway. Saw one man in front of him. The opposite of his messenger. Broad, tall was about all Konstantin got.

"You've been asking after someone," he said, low rumble.

"Yes."

"Man called Nikos. Bad teeth."

"That's the one."

"Why?"

"Helping a friend."

The man paused a moment, like 'friend' was an alien concept.

"I may be able to help," he said.

"Why?"

"He's treading on my toes. If anyone wants cash in this town, they come to me."

"Nikos is eating your lunch?"

"Yeah."

"New in the area, is he?"

The man shrugged. "Sort of. Thinks he can walk into my business, upset everything."

"So if I take him out no one will be upset?"

"Just the opposite."

"Good, that's all I wanted to know."

"If you do this you'll have me on your side. If you don't…"

Konstantin didn't reply. Was tired of the threats.

The big man turned to leave, said over his shoulder, "Come back here if you need anything. Ask for Ken."

Shorty grinned.

Striptease In Reverse

Fidelity had dressed as Nikos watched. Wouldn't leave her alone. Couldn't trust her, he claimed.

Yeah, right.

She'd pulled on jeans, slipped on a top. Didn't bother with a bra, the less time displaying skin the better.

Once there was nothing more to see, Nikos began searching her bedroom. Sniggered as he found her paraphernalia, said, "Is this what you bought with my money?"

Fidelity ignored him, tied her canvas shoes. Light, in case she needed to run again. Doubted she'd get the chance, but planned for the best anyway.

"What is it you call yourself, Plastic Fantastic?"

"You know it is."

"Looking at this lot, I can see where your name comes from."

She made no move to acknowledge his statement. Nikos didn't like that. He was the controlling type. Took one to know one.

"And men pay you good money to, what, abuse them?" Harder tone. Getting pissed off.

"If my job paid me well, then I wouldn't have needed to borrow anything from you."

Nikos laughed, said, "True. Okay, you're done now. We're leaving."

"I need a pee."

"Tough."

"Do you want me to piss myself in the back of your lovely car?"

Nikos thought about that, said, "Okay, but I'll be outside the door."

"If that's what turns you on."

Didn't like that either, spat, "I'm not one of your weirdo clients."

Fidelity suppressed a smirk, small successes, went into the bathroom, pulled down her pants, sat. Leant over and pushed

73

the door partly closed, even though Nikos had his back to her. After a couple of moments she stood. Took a lipstick from her pocket. Applied some to her lips. Wrote on the mirror. Flushed. Washed her hands. Had the cabinet open when Nikos entered. Put the make-up inside.

"Nice," he said. "But no more time-wasting. I assume you'll want your stuff."

She nodded. Was handed a carrier bag. Emptied the cabinet. Left it open. Allowed herself to be yanked out. Hoped the message would be enough. Needed Konstantin to get her out of this shit.

Or she was more than likely dead.

Lipstick Smile

Konstantin tried the handle. It was unlocked. Door swung back all the way. Small place, quick to search. Kitchen and living room downstairs, bedroom and bathroom up. Bereft of life, but no bodies. All looked okay, but didn't feel right.

Started over, dropped back down to the ground floor. Went through each space methodically.

Kitchen. Nothing.

Living room. Ditto.

Bedroom. Found it. Cupboards bare. No clothes within. Emptied in a hurry. Hangers on the floor. Opened drawers. Void too.

Bathroom. Towel slung over the side of the bath. Damp to the touch. No wet footprints on the floor.

Noticed cabinet was open. Pushed it closed. Saw 'Nikos' written in red lipstick. Sad face drawn in the 'O'.

Needed transport to get back to the loan shark's house. Remembered he'd dumped the wheels.

Swore he was going to get his own vehicle. Tomorrow. Stuff to do first.

Spotted a newspaper. Headline and photo that intrigued him. Would like to think that all the pieces fell into place. But would have been a lie. If anything, the picture was messier now.

Punchbag

"You've a choice," Nikos said.

"Really?" Fidelity replied. "Doesn't feel like it." Sat on a hard chair. Ropes tying her down would do that to a girl.

"You could really do with dropping the sarcasm," Nikos advised.

She shrugged. "Can't help it."

"After what I've got planned for your beautiful little self, you may change your mind."

"I doubt it," she said, tougher than she felt.

He laughed, said, "So, choices. Either, you pay me what you owe, which has increased considerably."

"I've already told you, I can't pay you any more than I originally borrowed."

He shrugged. "Not my problem."

"Or?"

"You work for me."

She didn't like the sound of that. Hadn't from the first time he'd suggested it. Which had put the whole subsequent plan into motion. At the time it had seemed like a good idea. Now it was utterly derailed. Smashed into bits.

"Meaning?"

"You'll like this," he said. Clearly she wouldn't. "I've a friend up town. He has a couple of houses. Where girls like you entertain men."

"I hardly entertain."

Carried on as if she hadn't spoken. "But he doesn't have anyone like you." Grabbed her face, squeezed her cheeks between his fingers. She tried not to show the pain. "You'll make us a fortune. Soon pay back your debt. Then it's quids in for a few years. 'Til you're worn out, that is."

He let go. Left red marks where he'd pressed hard. Her heart flexed. Hated someone else being in dominance. That hadn't happened since she was a teenager. Didn't know how the hell she was going to get out of this. Swore the next time Nikos came close she was going to kick him in the bollocks. No matter what it cost her.

"Time to make a decision," Nikos said. Huge grin on his face. Like he knew there was only one option.

"Fuck you."

"Fine. You can stay there until morning. But first... let's have ourselves a little fun."

Rust Bucket

Back at the club, Konstantin asked for Ken. Leaned in over the bar, shouted at the young guy pouring pints. Received a shrug in response. He stood there, blocking the way for the under-aged demanding drinks. Loud shouts over the music. Revelry. So-called enjoyment. Did nothing for the Russian.

In five minutes the wiry short guy was by his side. Said, "What do you want?"

"It's what I can tell you," Konstantin replied. No way anyone was monitoring this conversation. Dark, noisy.

Ken raised an unimpressed eyebrow.

"Where Nikos lives."

Short bark of a laugh from Ken. "Do you think we don't already know that?"

"But your boss said to come back when I knew where he was."

"No, you need to take the guy out."

"Do your dirty work for you."

Ken shrugged. "If you say so."

"I need transport."

"You don't have a car?" Ken was incredulous.

Konstantin's turn to shrug.

Ken shook his head. Pulled a key fob out of his pocket. Gave it to Konstantin. Then handed over a phone, said, "Call me when you're done."

Konstantin glanced at the contacts list. Only one number registered. When he looked back up, the man was lost in the bodies. Filtered into the crowd.

He found it out the rear of the club. Could barely be described as a car – it looked totally knackered. Rust coloured because that's all it was. Rubbish threatened to bury the vehicle. Looked like it hadn't moved for months. He wiped at the windows, looked inside. The interior was filled with junk too. Nevertheless it was locked. That made Konstantin pause. Opened the boot. Several guns. Not so bad then.

Got in. Threw all the waste from inside to join the mess in the alley. Twisted the key. Amazed it actually started first time. Bit of a knocking from the engine. So he wouldn't be able to push it too hard. No car chases allowed.

Konstantin drove home. Emptied the vehicle of the weapons. Deposited them in the cellar. Kept one for himself. Ironically, a very old Makarov. Stripped it. Checked it would fire. Reassembled it. Took seconds. Grabbed a silencer too. Ready for Nikos.

He drew up near the loan shark's pad. Got out. Checked the area out. Hoped he wasn't too late. Saw Nikos' vehicle was parked up. The house looked occupied. Lights on, movement within.

Went back to the junker. Drove a few yards so he had the front door in sight. Wasn't bothered whether Nikos would see him. Windows were so dirty. As effective as having them blacked out.

Sat back. Waited. Watched.

Knew it was better to hold back than rush in.

For now.

Hoped Fidelity was fine, but knew she probably wasn't. He felt bad.

Going Up Town

He waited all night, half dozed in the uncomfortable seat until they emerged into the early morning sun.

Slumped down he watched the heavies carry a bundle down the steps, deposit it in the boot. Disappointed to see it was a roll of carpet. No finesse. Konstantin was pretty certain what (or more accurately who) was contained within.

The pair waited outside for Nikos to descend. Opened the rear door for him. They got in the front. The Bentley glided away from the kerb. Konstantin started the engine.

He followed, kept a distance and, where possible, several vehicles between them. He remembered to check the petrol gauge and received a momentary shock when he saw the needle was firmly below empty. Tapped the facia, it didn't move. It was so empty his car should have been moving on fumes. Konstantin shrugged, had to hope it was simply broken.

Nikos headed out of Margate and was soon on an empty dual carriageway which cut through the marshland that had once been sea. The Bentley kept at a steady 70mph, so did Konstantin. He backed off.

After over an hour's uneventful driving they hit the A2 into London. The traffic was noticeably heavier, Konstantin closed the gap to a couple of cars. He had no idea where he was. Soon the Bentley took an exit ramp, entered urban streets that became narrower and more residential. Eventually parked. A decent tree-lined avenue, large houses over several floors. Fat, wealthy, privileged.

Konstantin dumped the rust bucket on double yellows a few yards away, but the other side of the road from Nikos. Stayed inside. Watched the loan shark go to a front door, ring the bell. Shook hands, entered.

The Russian climbed out, one hand inside his jacket clasped around the Makarov. He crossed but stayed on the road, ambled slowly towards the Bentley, glanced inside as he passed. Saw the heavies seated in the front. He stopped, bent down, knocked on the window and smiled. The heavy nearest him glared. Konstantin knocked again, still smiling.

The window wound down. "What the fuck do you want?" Thick Newcastle accent.

"I'm a bit lost," Konstantin said. "I was wondering if you could give me directions."

"You what?"

Without warning, Konstantin smashed the heavy in the mouth with the butt of the Makarov. Heard a couple of teeth break. Blood sprayed. Konstantin hit him on the neck as hard as he could. He slumped forward onto the steering wheel, out of it. Konstantin already had the barrel pointed at his colleague's forehead.

"Do not move an inch," he said. "Hands on the dashboard." Kept the gun on the heavy as Konstantin climbed into the back, watched closely for any sudden movement. None came. He pulled the door to, but not fully.

"Take out your gun with two fingers, drop it back here," Konstantin said.

"I'm not armed."

Konstantin eyed him. The heavy blinked, then complied. Konstantin pocketed the heavy weapon. Pulled the silencer out of his pocket, began to screw it into the Makarov's barrel while looking at the heavy. "You have a choice right now. I'm not interested in you or your friend. Just your boss. You can walk or I can kill you."

Nikos came out of the house then, bounded towards the car. Pulled open the door said, "Come on you fuckwits, why haven't you brought the girl in yet?"

The heavy pointed to the rear. Nikos saw the gun and Konstantin's grimace. Blanched.

"Get in," Konstantin ordered, swivelled the silenced barrel onto Nikos. Said to the heavy, "Time to choose."

Nikos figured out what was going on, said, "I'll double your pay."

The man looked at Konstantin over his shoulder, locked eyes. Saw the resolve and made a decision.

"Nothing's worth getting killed for."

Konstantin nodded. "Okay, get out, slowly. Walk away and keep going."

The heavy nodded, left the door open, strode up the leafy avenue, turned a corner and was gone.

"Just the pair of us now."

"You've just made a huge mistake," Nikos said.

Konstantin shook his head. "No, you did when you took Fidelity."

"I'm well connected. I'll come after you, I promise."

"You know a guy called Ken?"

Nikos paused at that, the colour dripped out of his face. "What do you want?"

Konstantin ignored him. "What is this place?"

"It belongs to someone I know."

The Russian sighed. Lowered the gun, pressed the barrel above Nikos' knee. "If I have to ask again I'll give you a permanent limp."

Nikos swallowed, closed his eyes. Whispered, "It's a brothel. Exclusive place. Caters to some unusual tastes."

"And what were you going to do with Fidelity?"

"Give her to the proprietor. She owes me money." Like that justified it.

Something clicked inside. Konstantin had to fight hard to stay his finger. Was seriously tempted to put a bullet in the guy's head. Wished he had, several years ago in a different time, but frighteningly similar place.

"What's his name? The owner." Ground the words out through his teeth.

"James."

Punched Nikos hard instead of using the gun. His head smacked off the window, out like a light. Konstantin breathed deeply to bring his heart rate down. He needed to be calm.

Got out of the car. Took the keys from the ignition. Opened the boot, undid the carpet roll. Fidelity was face down, he pulled her onto her back. Her chest rose and fell slowly. Looked like she was drugged.

Konstantin glanced up and down the street. No one in sight. He picked her up, carried her to the old banger. Lay her on the back seat. Opened the boot. Went back to get Nikos. Dumped him in the cramped space, slammed the lid down. Returned to the house.

Rang the bell.

Tear Me Up, Burn Me Down

He heard footsteps. The door, painted a lustrous black, opened inwards. A woman. Conservatively dressed, middle aged, stunningly beautiful.

"May I help you?" she asked.

"I'm here to see James about his latest acquisition. I'm a friend of Nikos'."

The woman looked puzzled, but beckoned Konstantin inside. Led him up several flights of stairs. The place was expensively decorated. Deep carpets, heavy wood, fine art. She stopped outside another closed door. Knocked, held it open for him without waiting for an answer. Konstantin entered.

A well-dressed guy was sprawled on a sofa. Sharp trousers and shirt. Plenty of gold visible. Well-tanned. Flicked a lighter, gold also, and lit a cigarette. Konstantin hated him immediately.

"James?"

"Yeah," he said, took a heavy drag. Broad London accent. "Where's Nikos?"

Konstantin took a couple of quick steps across the room, punched James hard in the face. The cigarette flew a few feet up in the air. Blood spurted from the guy's nose. Konstantin pulled James onto the floor, kicked him in the ribs a couple of times. Rammed the barrel of his gun under the pimp's jaw. Forced his head back. Saw the grimace of pain. Konstantin thought it the least he deserved.

"Nikos told me all about you," Konstantin said. "What you get up to here."

James shrugged, said, "It's just business."

Konstantin smacked him in the kidneys. "Bullshit."

"Tell that to the girls. They love it." James laughed until Konstantin rammed his head into the parquet a couple of times. Checked his pulse. Strong, but he'd be out for a while. Long enough.

Konstantin picked up the phone. Made a call to the police. He was sure they'd be interested in this place, but, once he'd replaced the receiver, decided to give some extra impetus in their headlong rush.

He left the room, brushed past the woman. "James said he isn't to be disturbed."

She shrugged.

Down the stairs, pulled some curtains off a rail. Heavy material, they'd be suitable. Outside on the pavement again, Konstantin went to the Bentley. The heavy was gone. Perhaps his friend had got him out. Konstantin didn't care. He opened the petrol cap. Stuffed the rag inside, dragged it out, felt it was soaked through. Held James' lighter to the rag until it caught, began to burn. A momentary regret. Konstantin needed transport, but the Bentley was simply too ostentatious.

He walked across the road, slid in behind the wheel. Was a hundred yards down the road when the Bentley exploded. Knew that would bring the police running.

The Delivery

Fidelity was still groggy when Konstantin carried her inside. He laid her on his own bed. Covered her up. Told the dominatrix he'd be fifteen minutes, but she was already asleep.

Back at the club, Konstantin parked the banger where he'd found it. Heard a few kicks and shouts from the boot. Ignored them. Went inside.

The place was closed for business, empty. One guy sweeping up. Konstantin asked for Ken, waited on the dance floor until he arrived. Handed over the keys.

"Well?" Ken asked.

"I've got him. He's in the car."

Ken grinned, said, "Well done."

Konstantin shrugged, wasn't interested in platitudes.

"What's next for Nikos?"

Ken smiled. "Nick you mean." Smiled at Konstantin's puzzlement. "An ex-employee, thought he had something on the boss, tried to muscle in on our game. This whole Nikos stuff is just a front, same as his fake tan. We'll sort him out, don't you worry. He won't be heard of again."

"Okay."

"Does that bother you?"

Konstantin thought about what could have become of Fidelity, said, "Not in the slightest."

Ken laughed. "You're a hard-nosed bastard."

"I took the guns out of the boot. Didn't want to get caught with them."

"Keep 'em if you want."

"I need one favour though."

"What?"

"A lift."

"You really need some wheels of your own."

"I know."

I Need A Holiday…

Fidelity's eyes fluttered open. She took a moment to focus on her surroundings, didn't recognise them, experienced a moment's panic when she recalled Nikos' threat. Then the snatched memory of Konstantin's intervention flooded into her mind and she lay back.

She ached all over. Had really taken a beating this time at the loan shark's hands. Bruises everywhere, a couple of cigarette burns, pounding headache. Only skin deep though. At least it hadn't got sexual. That would have been difficult to recover from a second time.

She tried to get out of bed, felt as weak as a kitten. Slumped back on the pillow.

The door opened then and Konstantin entered.

"How are you feeling?" he asked. Passed her a mug of something hot and steaming.

She tasted it, pulled a face. "Yuck."

"I thought you liked coffee?" he asked.

"No alcohol in it. Sorry, that was rude."

"No matter."

"What happened?"

"Not much."

Fidelity rolled her eyes. "You men, always the same. Understated one minute, over the top the next."

"Nikos won't be a problem any more," he said.

"Good."

"So, you owe me an explanation."

"What about?" Fidelity attempted innocence. Didn't work, clearly.

"Councillor Spray."

"Who?"

Konstantin put the newspaper he'd found next to her on the bed. Fidelity didn't need to look at it, knew exactly what it said.

"Busted."

"Looks like it."

"I didn't intend it to work out this way."

"We never do."

She sighed. "Richard was a client of mine, he wanted to help in any way he could, desperate to really. He was spearheading the clampdown on slum landlords and drugs and basically I asked him to add your house to the list."

"Why?"

"So you'd be forced to get involved."

"You could have just asked."

"Do you know how many times in my life when I've asked a man for help, they've wanted something in return that I'm just not prepared to give?"

"No."

"Too many. More than I could possibly count."

"I'm not like that."

"Perhaps, but how was I to know?"

"Fair enough."

"I'll get your house taken off the list."

"Thanks."

They were silent for a few minutes, each with their own thoughts.

"What's next?" Konstantin asked.

"I need a holiday."

"Me too."

"Get yourself some transport and take me somewhere."

"Deal."

Fat
Gary

Sick Note

Konstantin Boryakov ground his teeth. He'd been doing that a lot recently. Registered the calling of his name. For the third time in as many minutes. With a sigh he pushed himself to his feet, tried hard not to stamp up the stairs.

Didn't succeed.

"About fucking time," said Fidelity Brown.

She was sat up in bed, specifically *his* bed. Several large pillows enveloping her, cloak-like. She looked comfortable. And pale, in need of sunlight. Greasy hair, no make-up, thin T-shirt covering her ample chest.

"What this time?" asked Konstantin. He was tired, hadn't been sleeping well. Only one bed in the house as he'd never planned to have guests. Ever. Mind you, Fidelity was more of a patient. And he was a poor nurse. Dreadful bedside manner. Compassion had largely burned out a couple of days ago because he suspected Fidelity was milking the situation.

"I could do with a beer," she said.

"You're in recovery after beating. Alcohol won't do any good."

"Lying around here isn't either," she retorted.

"Either way, answer no. I bring you some water."

Fidelity huffed. Grabbed a pack of cigarettes from the bedside cabinet.

"I already asked several times, you not smoke in here," he said.

"Christ, you're like my father."

"Thankfully I not."

She pushed the covers off, swung her bare legs out of bed, planted her feet on the floor. Then tried to stand. She hissed in pain, sank back onto the bed. Konstantin felt a pang of pity, went over to help her up.

Fidelity brushed his hand away, said hard as a claw hammer, "I can do it myself."

"Fine." Konstantin left the room. A moment later he heard the window squeak, the strike of a match, heavy inhalation and a sigh. He shook his head.

Decided he needed to do something. Probably had some mail to collect. Left the house for the Post Office.

And that was what started it.

The Snoop

Fidelity heard the front door close. Craned her head out of the window and saw Konstantin's retreating back. She shook her head, annoyed at herself for pushing him so hard. But couldn't help it. She found it difficult to trust anyone, but particularly men.

She binned the fag out the window, watched it arc downwards a couple of floors. Hit a mangy black cat on the head. Stupid thing barely noticed. Fidelity glared at the bed, didn't like the idea of getting back in, as yielding as it was. And she was up now, decided some exercise would be good. Start getting her strength back.

A lengthy limp across the room, opened the door, listened, wasn't sure why. She didn't hear anything. Found herself on a narrow landing, knew the bathroom was immediately opposite, but wasn't interested in going somewhere familiar. Two more doors held her attention. Both were locked. Rattling the handle made no difference to their reluctance to reveal their innards.

The stairs. They'd be a challenge. She leant against the wall, went down crab-wise, one foot and one step at a time.

Same story in the hallway. It was dim, very little natural light. All the doors closed and secured, except into the kitchen. Cold vinyl floor, plain brown fascia. Basic and functional. She looked through the cupboards, didn't find anything out of the ordinary. Food in the fridge, all the pots and pans washed up, cutlery arranged in straight lines. Neat and tidy. Spick and span.

She did notice two things, however. The rear exit itself was thick, solid and metal lined as well as being locked and bolted. And there were bars on the window. Couldn't see anything outside because the glass was frosted.

Okay, she shrugged, *that was three things. Fuck it.*

Back in the hall Fidelity eyed the stairs. A mountain to climb. And for what? Not much. The only thing for sure – Konstantin was an extremely private man. She put her foot on the bottom step. Began the slow, difficult ascent. Her Sherpa Tensing had left the building.

Black Mail

The key turned easily. Gave access to a small space, a shelf really. But it didn't need to be large because Konstantin didn't receive much mail. Whatever he collected was official. Such as an electoral registration form despatched to 'The Occupier' or the occasional bill that needed paying. All sent to a different address up North, re-directed back here. So to all intents and purposes, no one was recorded as residing at Konstantin's house.

Today was different, though. A large, cream coloured envelope sat at an angle across the opening. Konstantin eyed it, this unexpected and alien thing. Eventually he pulled it out, gripped between two fingers, like it was diseased. Stared at it. Heavy, expensive paper. Bold, cursive writing on the front. Business postmark, not a stamp. Dated almost a week ago. Sent by Wright & Partners. Didn't recognise them. Turned it over, no return address.

Nothing else inside the post box, Konstantin closed and locked it. Stuffed the envelope into a pocket and left. Went to a nearby café. Ordered espresso, took it and himself into a corner, away from everyone else.

He withdrew the envelope from his pocket, laid it on the table, address side up. Eyed it for a minute. Flipped it over, carefully peeled the flap open. Inside was a single sheet of the same expensive paper. Unfolded it, read the typed message. It didn't make sense. Nor did it the second time.

Thirty minutes later, Konstantin stood outside Wright & Partners. A narrow fronted building over several floors located at the top of Broadstairs High Street. Not the best site for passing trade. Looked relatively ordinary from the outside. Plain and in need of some upkeep.

He entered, discovered a decent-sized reception area. Again modest. Plenty of space, lots of natural light. Low table with some brochures on and a couple of chairs for visitors to wait. A middle-aged woman behind a desk, a few posters on the wall. She looked up, said, "Can I help you?"

Konstantin flicked his eyes to her. Dropped the Russian accent as he tended to do at times like these. "I received a letter."

"Okay."

"From Mr. Wright."

"That happens occasionally."

"He said I needed to contact him."

"Well he's not here right now. Mr. Wright is based in our Canterbury office. You'll need to make an appointment."

"Fine. Tell him I'll be here at 9am tomorrow."

The receptionist laughed, incredulity a stripe throughout, said, "I'm afraid that won't be possible, sir. Mr. Wright has a very full schedule. It will take days before he can be available."

"Tell him Paul Black will be here at 9am. Either he sees me then, or not at all."

"Sir, I say again that will simply prove impossible," she spluttered, all humour in her tone strangled at birth.

Konstantin shrugged. "Not my problem. See you tomorrow."

He left the woman staring open mouthed. At the exit Konstantin grabbed a brochure from the table. Once outside he pulled his mobile from a pocket, stabbed at the keys. When it connected, said, "Can I speak to Mr. Wright please?"

"I'm afraid he's out at a lunch appointment right now."

Konstantin looked at his watch. 11am.

"When will he be back?"

"I don't know, his diary is blocked out all day."

"But he will be returning?"

"I'm sure, yes."

Konstantin disconnected.

A short walk up the hill brought Konstantin to the station. Just two platforms, one either side of a double track. Checked out the schedule, bought a return ticket to Canterbury, only had to wait nine minutes.

When the clunker arrived he climbed aboard, found a seat. Read the brochure he'd picked up, stared out the window during the half hour journey. Watched the houses and trees flick lazily by. High speed it was not.

When the train finally reached its destination, Konstantin followed the small crowd out the station. On an exterior wall he read a small plaque proclaiming that the first passenger rail railway in the world operated from this station in 1830. Shrugged. Ancient history. Began the trek into town.

Konstantin discovered the head office of Wright & Partners tucked off the main pedestrian drag, a relatively quiet street mere yards away from the hubbub of serious shoppers and casual coffee drinkers. It was an old, red brick building that spoke of money, permanence and influence.

He rang the number again, asked if Wright was back yet. Received a negative response. Went back around the corner to a market stall. Bought some cheap items of clothing and a rucksack.

Took only a minute. He sank into a doorway near the office, stood in the shadows and waited.

It was nearing 2pm by the time Neil Wright, senior partner, returned. Konstantin recognised him from the brochure. Distinguished, fit, sharp. Not someone who regularly partook of three hour lunch breaks. Expensive suit, carried a slim briefcase in one hand, in the other a phone, pressed to his ear. Distracted. Perfect.

Konstantin pulled a hat low over his eyes, tucked his hair underneath. Slotted on sunglasses, pulled a scarf over the bottom of his face to cover his beard.

Stepped out into the sunlight, walked quickly towards Wright who was too busy with his call to notice the world. Shoulder-barged him. The phone flew out of the lawyer's hand. Konstantin grabbed at the man's wrist holding the briefcase. Squeezed hard. Wright shrieked, let go. Konstantin took the case, then pushed the man over his outstretched foot. Wright hit the ground hard. It was all done in seconds.

Konstantin strode off, bent briefly to grab the spilled phone. Didn't look back, shoved the briefcase into a carrier bag turned inside out so no logo was visible. Pulled the scarf down off his face so he didn't attract attention. Was around the corner before Wright could react. He merged into the teeming pedestrians.

Headed to the nearest large department store. Up three floors to the public toilets. Grabbed a jacket as he went past a rack. Went inside a stall. Dropped the lid on the toilet, placed the briefcase on it.

Tried the catches. Locked. Insufficient time available to break them so it went back into the bag.

Konstantin switched jackets, shoved his into the bag as well. Wasn't giving up his leather for anyone. Tore the security tags off before he shrugged it on. Changed hat and sunglasses too. All he could do in a short space of time.

Flushed, exited the stall then re-joined the throng. Kept his head down so any CCTV wouldn't register his features, hidden by the wide brim too. Left the store by a different entrance and walked a circuitous route along back roads to the station. He arrived just as a train was drawing up, as planned. He stepped aboard, settled back. Hadn't caught sight of a policeman once. Allowed himself the briefest of smiles.

Wright and Wrong

Neil Wright stormed into his office, brushed off the irritatingly wittering attentions of his secretary. Slammed the door shut and flopped down into his swivel chair. He looked out the window a moment, stared at a gargoyle affixed to the building opposite. Attempted to calm down as he ran over the events of his mugging again.

On the floor in a heartbeat and by the time the lawyer had got off his backside his attacker was long gone. His main impression had been bulk. The guy literally blocked the light out as he'd loomed over. When he'd reached the main street his attacker was out of sight, merged into the random bodies out spending cash. Neil wasn't a tall man so he'd struggled to see over everyone's heads.

The problem was he had the case. The fucking case was gone! Which was potentially a huge problem. There were several items within that were worthless at face value, but priceless for their content. If they found their way to the wrong people... He'd be dead.

And that was the knotty problem Wright couldn't unravel. Was it a random robbery? Purely opportunistic? Or had he been targeted?

However, he really only had one decision to make. Whether to ring his client or not. His hand hovered over the telephone. Then he pulled it back, decided it was best to wait twenty four hours. Because once this little cat was out the bag there was no stuffing it back in.

The phone rang. Made his heart leap. A single tone, internal. He let out a huge sigh. Picked it up. Listened as his secretary told him about the demand made by a man called Paul Black to see him at 9am tomorrow.

"Okay, cancel my morning appointments."

"But, sir..."

"I'm aware who I'm supposed to be seeing, please just do it."

"Yes, Mr. Wright."

Neil sat back in his chair. At least one thing had gone to plan today. He opened a drawer, poured himself a slug of brandy into a crystal glass. Threw it down his throat. Revelled in the burn, enjoyed the impact on the pit of his stomach, the almost immediate croon of alcohol in his blood.

Picked up the receiver again, dialled Fat Gary's number, said, "He's made contact. I'm seeing him tomorrow at my Broadstairs office."

"Already? I'm in fucking Liverpool!" shouted Fat Gary in a broad Scouse accent.

"He didn't give me any choice."

"Change the appointment."

"I can't. I've no way of getting in touch with him quickly enough. You'll have to come down. Now."

"Great, thanks pal. I'd best get my arse moving then," said Fat Gary sarcastically.

"See you tomorrow."

"You won't."

Neil heard the line disconnect.

Didn't even get a 'thank you' from the fat fuck.

The Case

Konstantin unlocked the back door to his home. Stepped inside. Listened for a moment. It was totally silent. Left the briefcase downstairs, checked on Fidelity. She was flat out. Mouth open, one slim leg hanging off the bed.

He made a cup of coffee, then went into the small tool room he was in the process of setting up. Locked the door behind him. Put the briefcase on a bench, selected a small screwdriver and attacked the catches. It didn't take much to break them. Made for show, not strength.

Konstantin lifted the lid. Inside were several files. He picked them up. Flicked through. Innocuous enough. Looked like property deals. Somebody was making money, the other party losing. But that was always the way.

He tipped everything out of the case onto the bench. Felt around the lining, it was a soft, beige leather. Almost missed it. A well concealed flap. Tugged at it and revealed a hidden compartment in the base. Inside was a single sheet of paper. The contents meant absolutely nothing to Konstantin. But they were clearly important, otherwise they wouldn't be concealed.

Turned his attention to the phone. It was locked with a pass code. Konstantin needed a little time to gain access. He hooked the mobile up to his PC, clicked on a piece of software. Plugged the phone in via a USB cable. The computer found the device and started the hunt for the correct four number combination. It didn't take long, relatively few variables to compare.

He went to the text list. It was empty. Same with e-mail and the contacts. Blank. Totally blank. Just the one number in the call list, which had to be the one he was on at the time Konstantin appropriated the briefcase. He rang it. A voice told Konstantin the number didn't exist. Disconnected. More than likely a throw-away single use unit. A dead end.

He sighed. Shook his head at the thumping from upstairs. Fidelity.

"What?"

"That's no way to speak to a recuperating guest," Fidelity pouted. She was sat up in bed, covers pushed down beneath her knickers.

Konstantin shrugged. "You seem well enough to me."

Fidelity's eyes narrowed. "Well enough for what?"

"To stop dragging me around like wet nurse."

"That's not it. I know what you're thinking," she said, daggers in her tone. "You're expecting a reward for you helping me."

"What?" Konstantin didn't have a clue what she was talking about, was taken by surprise in the change of her tone.

"You men are all the same. Give a little, take a lot. Well come on then baby, I'm all yours!"

She kicked the covers off, lay out on the bed, flung her arms and legs wide.

Suddenly it dawned on Konstantin what 'a lot' meant. Anger flared within, the worst kind. He spun on his heel, left the bedroom. Slammed the door hard behind him.

Fidelity sat up, realised she might have misjudged the situation.

A Vodka Fuelled Punch-Up

Fury burned through Konstantin like molten lava. He could feel the heat in his heart, pumping anger through his veins. Only one thing he could do to douse the burn.

Drink. And heavily.

He stormed out of the house, to the nearest pub. Ordered vodka. Lost his temper when the barman said they were out. Grabbed the guy by the shirt, dragged him over the damp bar. Sent glasses spilling. Growled in his face, then saw the abject fear there.

The Russian let go of him, left the man hanging over the broad wooden expanse. Legs and arms either side like a puppet with its strings cut. Turned and walked out.

Headed to the shittiest pub in Margate he could think of. The one where there were always fights. So anyone he punched would be a legit target, not some poor kid earning minimum wage, stinking of stale beer and fried food.

Found the place, pushed the door open. It was loud. Pumping music, regulars shouting over the noise to make themselves heard. Just made it worse and fed back on itself. The sweet smell of cannabis in the air. Pushed his way to the bar, faced down the looks he received. Challenge all over his face. He got left alone. Not enough alcoholic courage imbibed yet.

Finally he got vodka. A double. Then several more. Stayed standing at the bar the whole while. A rock around which lesser men ebbed and flowed.

It took several hours for it to kick off. Nearing closing time for the pubs. But opening time for the clubs. So the pissheads could carry on. Like they needed to.

Konstantin received a tap on the shoulder. Ignored it.

"'Ere mate. I'm talking to you." Reedy voice which went unheeded.

A push on the shoulder. "Oi, wanker. I don't like someone having their back to me. Freaks me out."

Konstantin smiled to himself. Looked over his shoulder. Saw a little Chinese guy. Tattoos everywhere. Vest. Black trousers. Trying to look like Bruce Lee. His fists were clenched. A fag hung out of his lips, smoke curled upwards. So much for the smoking ban.

"Not my problem," said Konstantin. Went back to his drink.

"It soon fucking will be unless you *turn around*."

The Russian threw back the rest of his vodka. It tasted like water, probably was. Had the same effect. Slowly pirouetted. Rolled his neck and shoulders. Cracked his knuckles. Ordinarily Konstantin didn't do showy stuff. But for this prick…

"Fucking wise move fella," said the Chinese guy. Then received a mouthful of knuckles. Compressed the fag against his lips. Konstantin felt blood spray over his fist, had already followed up with a punch to the solar plexus. Enjoyed the 'oof' as the guy's lungs urgently expelled the breath they held. He hit the deck, hard. Konstantin stamped on his right hand. Heard a crunch like biting into a crisp, then a scream.

Konstantin looked up. He hadn't broken sweat. The pub was silent except for the Chinese guy moaning pathetically. Even the pounding music had been turned off.

Then all hell broke loose…

Gregory's Deal

The room was small, claustrophobic. Just him, two chairs, a table and a single CCTV camera high up where wall kissed ceiling. There was a bright red dot of light on the camera's casing. Neutral colours. Dull. Almost a cell. The door was locked in any case. Konstantin faced it, occupied one of the chairs. Kept his back to the wall.

He sighed, but stayed seated. Konstantin wasn't going to demonstrate any outward signs of irritation like pacing the floor or fidgeting. He wouldn't give them the pleasure. He kept his hands clasped in front of him on the table in full view. The skinned knuckles still tingled. Konstantin knew he'd been stupid, would probably have a record now, but he'd handle the self-recrimination later.

The light on the camera went out. One moment it was there, the next the illumination disappeared. More violence required then, probably. That was fine by him. Got ready for it.

Only a few seconds later the door was unlocked, swung inwards. A single man entered, shut the door behind him. Already unusual. No accompanying constable. The guy looked tired, bags under his eyes, dark hair a mess. He was in plain clothes, but dressed relatively well. Shirt open at the neck, tie missing. Like he'd had a long night.

The detective put a manila file on the table. Then pulled the chair back, lowered himself down, looked into Konstantin's eyes. Sighed and shook his head. The Russian waited for the other to speak. No way was he breaking the silence first.

"So, Mr. No Name, what were you doing in The English Flag earlier this evening?"

Konstantin had so far refused to give any personal details, simply clammed up. He said, "Drinking."

That much of an admission was okay. He reeked of alcohol and had been arrested on the premises.

"I'd been told you weren't being very co-operative by my colleagues. Seems they were right."

Konstantin retained his poker face. Didn't bother shrugging. It would be a waste of energy.

The cop continued, "I assume you're wondering why I had the camera turned off?" Konstantin did shrug this time. "Well, it was because of a tramp."

"I don't understand," said Konstantin, because he didn't. Concern and query made his adrenaline kick up another notch.

"Ah, you do speak more than one word at a time then." The cop smiled with the minor triumph. "You don't remember me, do you?"

"Should I?"

"I'm DC Gregory."

A dim light of memory flickered in Konstantin's mind. He nodded.

"Good," said Gregory.

"What do you want?"

"I'm going to help you."

"And in return I give, what?" Konstantin recoiled inside, knowing he sounded like Fidelity had earlier today.

"Nothing. This is simply payback for you helping Ralph. He was my friend. You were there for him when no one else was. Not even me."

The Russian let the surprise play across his features. He was bone tired, had been awake all night.

Gregory held the file up, said, "This is your arrest record and photo. They'll disappear as soon as you leave the building. It'll be like you never existed."

A shiver hit Konstantin. Words from the past back to haunt him again. Incredible how history repeated itself.

"Thank you."

"No need. Just make sure this is the last time we meet under these circumstances. I won't be able or willing to pull this trick a second time."

Konstantin nodded.

"Good," said Gregory. He escorted Konstantin out of the building, signing him out first and returning the Russian's meagre belongings.

"What time is it?" asked Konstantin as he blinked in the morning sunlight.

The cop flicked a glance at his watch, said, "Just after 8am. Got somewhere to be?"

"No," lied Konstantin. "Just wondering how long before the pub opens."

"Very funny. Hope not to see you around." Gregory spun on his heel and went back into the police station.

"Yeah, yeah," said Konstantin to the man's back.

Less than an hour before his appointment with the lawyer. There was no way Konstantin could get home, shower and change by then. So he had two choices. Train or taxi.

A quick assessment of his financial situation made the decision for him. He began the walk along Margate sea front. Knew he needed to ensure he didn't fall asleep once aboard the train and it was rocking him like a baby.

In a moment of honest reflection, Konstantin decided that the fight with the Bruce Lee wannabe hadn't sated his anger. Another rumble was required. But he couldn't see the soft skinned solicitor providing him the outlet he needed.

Konstantin couldn't have been further from the truth.

Guilty Displeasures

Fidelity had stayed awake most of the night waiting for Konstantin to come back. Every time she'd nodded off, Fidelity awoke with a jerk. She pinched herself, opened the window, left the covers off the bed. Anything to remain conscious.

Which, she decided when she came to with the sun streaming into the room, had proved an entirely unsuccessful tactic.

Fidelity swung her feet onto the floor, hissed. Pushed herself up onto them and shuffled across the sanded floorboards. The door was wide open, the way she'd left it. Poked her head out cautiously, like it was going to get shot off. Not a sound.

She listened at Konstantin's door, ear pressed against the rough wood. Couldn't hear anything. Knew he was a light sleeper, but nevertheless. Knocked. Waited. Tried the handle. Locked.

Back against the wall, she slid down the stairs one at a time in a repeat of yesterday's action, although she was a little faster this time. Maybe she was knitting together at last. Fucking hoped so.

Her soles landed on cold tiles. Just the hum of the fridge for company. Was surprised to see one of the rooms was open for access, the door back on its hinges. Which meant Konstantin was in the house after all.

Decided against calling out his name, and went into the kitchen instead. Rustled up a coffee the way she knew he liked it. Carried the steaming mug into the living room.

Empty. Of Konstantin anyway. Sparsely furnished otherwise. But that wasn't what interested her.

She walked across the room to the roughly hewn entrance in the far wall. It led into a tool room. A bench with a powerful light overhead. Several vices of different sizes affixed to it. An industrial drill, lots of tools on boards on the wall. There was the smell of gun oil in the air.

Fidelity put the mug down, went to the briefcase that lay on the bench. Noted the broken locks. Sifted through the boring contents. Couldn't believe it belonged to Konstantin. Then she saw the two pieces of paper. Looked like they'd been thrown down, left in a rush. Fidelity blushed. She knew why. It was her fault.

She found the letter addressed to Paul Black, a handwritten note in the corner. Time and place. There was a clock on the wall. Perhaps she'd be able to make it. Certainly couldn't take public transport, so a taxi then.

Fuck the expense.

Fat Gary pulled up outside the office. Stopped on double yellows. Flicked the switch that started the repetitive and irritating on-off flick of the hazard lights. He yawned. Tired, having driven through much of the night once he'd picked the lads up. Stupid bastards had been out on the piss. But at least the traffic had been light with the unseasonable hour.

He'd got a few hours' sleep in a lay-by just outside town. But now he ached all over, had a terrible taste in his furry mouth.

Wondered if he had chance to grab something from the shop opposite before his man turned up. Looked at the clock on the dashboard. Yeah, they had ten minutes.

"Tom," he said, poking one of his men in the ribs. "Go get us some chocolate from over there." He pointed at the newsagent behind a bus stop. Pushed a fiver into Tom's meaty hand. "And some crisps too. Just not cheese and onion. I fucking hate cheese and onion."

Tom shook his head, but got out the van. Stuck two fingers up at the driver of the car which almost ran him over.

Will Power

The receptionist glanced up as Konstantin entered Wright & Partners (Broadstairs). She glowered at him, remembering their encounter the previous day.

The journey over had been unmercifully short and jerky. No gentle acceleration and braking with this driver. Perhaps Lewis Hamilton was now working for South Eastern Trains.

"I've an appointment with…"

She cut him off, said, "Yes, yes I know." Picked up the phone, jabbed at the keypad. "He's here to see you sir… Okay, I'll show him up."

The receptionist sniffed, stood, smoothed down her skirt. Touched her hair to ensure it was still piled neatly on top of her head and pinned in place. Konstantin neglected to tell her she had lipstick on her teeth.

She opened the small gate to allow him through into her domain, led Konstantin up a narrow flight of stairs to the first floor. Several closed doors, she knocked on one.

"Enter."

She did, said, "Your visitor, sir."

"Thank you Evangeline," said Wright. He didn't rise in greeting.

"Do you need anything else?"

"No, I don't think so. We'll be brief."

She left, closed the door gently behind her. Konstantin listened to the creaks of the steps as she descended.

The room was sparse, to say the least. A desk, two chairs, a few bookshelves, boxes of files. Nothing personal on show. A large bay window looking out onto the High Street, two sashes yawning to allow a soft breeze in and the sound of traffic.

"Take a pew, would you?" Wright waved at the visitor's seat. No offering a hand to shake.

Konstantin tossed the letter on the desk. He disliked like the man's attitude, decided that two could more than happily play that game.

"You wrote to me."

"I did Mr. Black. Very observant of you." A silence ensued for a few moments. There was a dense air of distrust in the room.

"Are you going to tell me what this is about? You mentioned a will naming me as sole beneficiary of David Chester's estate."

"Yes, that. I have to apologise. There was a clerical error by one of my staff. You shouldn't have received that communication."

"So there is no David Chester."

"Not at all. He existed. It's just you weren't his beneficiary."

"So you've wasted my time."

"It seems so."

Konstantin sighed. Wondered what the hell was going on here but was too angry to assimilate his thoughts into a coherent decision.

He stood, said, "If ever I need a lawyer I'll know where not to come."

"Very droll. Would you mind seeing yourself out?"

Konstantin descended the stairs. Pushed past the receptionist without a word.

The Take Down (Or Not)

Neil stood up as soon as the man he knew as Paul Black left the room. Crossed to the bay, closed both windows, then drifted back into the shadows. Even though it went against his instincts, he'd been told to witness events outside. But that didn't mean he would be seen doing so. Neil had to stay clean in case matters got dirty.

"That's the signal," said Fat Gary in his heavier Scouse accent. "Get your fucking arses outside. No screw ups."

Konstantin hit the street. Had more questions than answers. He'd known the letter was bullshit, he just hadn't expected it to be quite as much of an anti-climax.

Something caught his eye, set an alarm bell clamouring inside his head. A white van, double yellows a few yards. Nothing unusual in that. It was expected in this country. Why bother having rules? The back doors were open, two men unloading boxes.

He stared at them a moment, worked out what was amiss. First, the newsagent was the other side of the road. And there was a space out the front. So they were parked in the wrong location. Who heard of a delivery guy deliberately making his job more difficult?

Second, the boxes were large and stacked, but the men weren't struggling with them. They looked as light as feathers. Empty. For show.

Then he caught a glance from one of the guys, most of his face hidden by a cap. But nevertheless, the guy had clocked him. Their eyes locked. Saw him swear.

Two choices. Walk. Confront.

He chose the latter, he needed to blow off some more steam. No pedestrians around, couple of cars on the road. Mid-week in a small seaside town.

Walked the few yards from the lawyer's entrance to the van. Arms loose, down by his side.

Everything went pear-shaped almost immediately. Konstantin got up close to the delivery guys, who forgot about their goods. Dropped the boxes to the ground.

Konstantin punched the first guy in the solar plexus. He folded over like tissue paper. Elbowed the other in the face as he came in. Konstantin heard the crunch of bone. Nose gone. Caught the first guy with an uppercut, under the chin. Teeth ground as bottom and top jaw met in a rush. Although the swing was shallow the guy lost consciousness, sagged to the floor. Brain decelerating against bone.

The one with the broken nose stepped up, gore masking the lower half of his face but couldn't cover the snarl. He was breathing heavily through his mouth, would be for a week or two until his beak recovered.

The Russian rolled his shoulders, beckoned the guy forward. Struck out with a couple of jabs, caught him on the side of the face. Konstantin avoided a wild haymaker, stepped inside the arc and put a couple of solid punches into his opponent's kidney. Then shoved a shoulder into him, smiled as he staggered back and hit the van. Leant on it for support.

"Come on," said Konstantin, "at least give me a half decent fight."

With a roar the bloodied man rushed at Konstantin, swinging. The Russian ducked under, smashed him in the balls. The guy's eyes bulged, sank to his knees. Konstantin cracked him on the back of the neck and he hit the deck face down.

"Clap, clap," said someone. Liverpudlian accent.

Looked up, saw the barrel of a gun gaping at him. Held rock steady, a fat bloke standing behind it. Balding, sallow skin, like all he ate was junk food. Maybe some of it smeared around his sneering mouth right now.

"Just so you know," he said, "this is for Dave."

"Who?"

He laughed, said, "You want to know how many times people deny knowing anything with a gun pointed at them?"

"Not really."

"Good, 'cos I hate small talk." The Scouser hefted the gun, aimed it at Konstantin's forehead.

Then the man's eyes rolled up into the back of his head and he toppled like a felled tree. Revealed Fidelity holding a lump of wood in her hand.

A bus rolled up then, drew to a halt at the stop opposite. Konstantin saw a smear of shocked faces pressed to the window.

"Come on," she said.

Five minutes later, Konstantin at the wheel, Fidelity in the passenger seat, they were rolling out of Broadstairs in Fat Gary's white van.

"We need to dump this," said Fidelity.

"What you doing here?" asked Konstantin.

Fidelity eyed him, said, "Thank you would work well right now."

"I had it handled."

"Really?" She arched an eyebrow.

"I just about to get information from him. And you spoiled it."

"Well fuck you very much," she said, turned and stared out the passenger window.

He twisted the wheel, turned into a large shopping centre. Lots of cars available to 'borrow'. He drove the van to the furthest point in the car park, left it across two bays in front of a closed casino. Konstantin got out, was several paces away before Fidelity could even move.

She followed painfully in his wake, watched him twist his head left, right. He walked diagonally across the space, threaded between vehicles. Stopped between a flatbed truck and a small coupé, the former blocking the view of any casual passer-by. Within seconds he was pulling open the door of the latter, parked his arse on the seat, bent down. Low screech as he yanked off the plastic cover beneath the steering wheel.

By the time Fidelity was at the car, the engine was running.

"Get in," said Konstantin.

She did. Slowly.

Not a word was spoken on the way back to Konstantin's pad.

Fat Gary's A Fuck Up

Neil watched the events unfold with open-mouthed shock. Once the fat fuck Gary hit the deck, felled by the slutty looking woman with the limp, he left the shadows. Grabbed his throwaway mobile off the desk, dialled a number.

Once it connected, said, "Frank, it's me. Gary screwed up. The take failed."

"What a fucking idiot."

The lawyer didn't answer, didn't need to, said, "I'm getting out of here."

"Sure."

"The police will be on their way. And an ambulance, I reckon."

Frank sighed. Neil could imagine his fingers, the size of healthy sausages, gripping the phone tightly. Imagined he could hear the creak of straining plastic.

"I'll see him in hospital then." With that, Frank ended the call.

The lawyer grabbed his briefcase and headed down the stairs as sirens did indeed enter earshot. In reception, he found Evangeline, if that was her real name, had already gone. Didn't matter. She was a stand-in hired for a couple of weeks. Probably slipped out when the trouble kicked off. Sensible girl.

He scooped up the handful of brochures on the table by the door, stuffed them into his pocket. Ripped the posters off the wall. Glanced around to ensure he'd missed nothing. Went to the rear entrance, stepped into an alley. Moments later he was in a quiet road and unlocking his car, a Jaguar. Patriotic and ostentatious in one. He pulled away and left Fat Gary to his own unconscious devices.

Frank McGavin shook his head. He'd known it was a mistake to let someone onto his patch to sort out a little problem. But he'd also known Fat Gary would have gone ahead whether Frank had agreed or not. Because he'd have done the same. Family was family, after all.

Fat Gary had put up the cash for the event. Frank had put up the lawyer. But then Fat Gary royally fucked a straightforward takedown by the sound of it. Sighed. Picked up the phone again, made a call.

"Ken, it's me. Look, some stuff has gone tits up. I need you to drop everything and get your arse to the hospital."

"Who's been done over boss?"

"Fat Gary."

"Fucking hell."

Frank waited for the 'I told you so'. But Ken was too wise for that.

"Find out what ward he's in, then keep an eye on who comes looking for him. I want to know who Fat Gary was after."

"He didn't tell you?"

"He didn't know."

"Fat and stupid then."

"Clearly. Call me when you've information."

"Okay boss."

Frank disconnected. Decided that Fat Gary's family would be losing another member. At least it'd keep the florists in Liverpool busy. His way of helping rebuild the economy.

Vacant Spaces

Konstantin stared at the building in the early morning light. All quiet. Stepped into the small front garden, looked through the window, placed a hand against the glass to shade his eyes. It was entirely empty. No receptionist behind the desk. Bare walls.

He tried the door handle. It was unlocked. Konstantin entered. There was a feeling of emptiness about the place. Abandonment. Went up the stairs, into the office the lawyer had occupied. As empty as a banker's brain. Stuck his head into the other rooms. Dust, cobwebs, piles of boxes. Hadn't been used properly for some time. It was simply a building to store junk.

"Anything?" asked Fidelity.

Konstantin shook his head. "Temporary office, just a set up."

"What next?"

"Canterbury."

By the time they reached Wright's head office, Konstantin was sick of Fidelity's complaining. About public transport, the weather, people. Anything and everything. But she shut up as soon as they found the same picture as Broadstairs.

The building was split between several firms. Some taking a single room, others a whole floor. Wright & Partners had a broom cupboard in comparison. Just an empty space, post shoved under the door. Konstantin could see a couple of envelope corners poking out. He snagged them with a fingernail. Standard junk. Nothing of value. Dropped them on the floor.

Konstantin crossed the corridor, entered a small room. It was an insurance company. One man band, literally.

A guy with a bland expression shrugged, "Never seen anyone use the place."

"How long has it been empty?" asked Konstantin.

"As long as I've been here."

Fidelity sighed, spat, "How fucking long is that?"

The guy eyed her with distaste, said to Konstantin, "Over two years."

"Thanks."

"No worries."

As they left Konstantin said, "Was that necessary?"

"The guy doesn't like women, it pissed me off."

"How could you tell?"

"When you've been around men in the way I have, it's easy to spot the types."

Konstantin didn't have an answer for that so stuck to saying nothing.

Back in the street Konstantin looked up at the building, said, "The lawyer must be around here somewhere. I hit him right on this spot."

"Must have been pure good luck."

"Maybe." But Konstantin didn't believe in luck. Too random an event for his liking.

"Have you tried calling them?"

"Yes. Disconnected."

"Must have been set up just for you. A temporary front."

"I expect so. The phone number is the same as on here." Konstantin passed her the brochure for Wright & Partners he'd picked up yesterday.

"Someone has gone to a lot of effort."

"Yes." Konstantin didn't like that little nugget. It meant whoever it was wouldn't stop until it was over. So he needed to ensure the other guy got ended first.

"Hospital next," he said.

Fidelity sighed, said, "You really need to get your own wheels."

"Too busy at the moment."

Konstantin smiled at the heavy sigh.

Visiting Hours Are Over

It didn't take Ken long to track down Fat Gary. The nearest hospital to where he'd been put into the back of an ambulance was Margate. The Queen Elizabeth the Queen Mother was a sprawling mish-mash of buildings. Old and older constructions jumbled together over a ridiculously large area. It would take a month of Sundays to search from top to bottom.

But Ken had contacts here. Plenty of stressed out doctors and nurses who were his customers. In regular need of a chemical upper. He had a couple of suppliers on site as well, providing all sorts of medical supplies the NHS 'lost'. Ken simply redistributed the waste. Like Frank, he was doing his bit for the wider society.

So a tenner to one of his nursing contacts, who took as many seconds to locate Fat Gary. Even down to the bed number. Twenty quid and he had a white lab coat and a badge. Another tenner secured a text whenever someone asked after Fat Gary at reception.

Ken took the long walk, he needed a map to get around. It always amazed him how free the general public was to wander around medical facilities, but even so if you had a white coat on, you were God.

Finally reached where he wanted. Checked the patient list on the large whiteboard at the nurse's station. There he was. Gary McSherry. Ken guessed his men would be close by. They were less of a concern, but would need to be cleared up should Frank decide to pull the trigger.

He entered the ward. Fat Gary was in the middle. Old geezers to his left and right.

"About fucking time," said Fat Gary when Ken reached the foot of his bed. He picked up the chart. Looked at the words and numbers written there, didn't have a clue what they meant.

"Hey, Doc. I'm speaking to you."

Ken brought his gaze onto Fat Gary. "What seems to be the problem?"

"It's this place." Gary waved an arm around. Flesh hung off the limb, like the skin had been stretched. A keep fit freak, it made Ken want to hurl. How could people let themselves go so much?

Gary was off again, said, "I shouldn't be in here. I want my own room. Not be stuck in here with these smelly bastards."

The old guy in the next bed farted and cackled.

"See what I mean?" said Fat Gary.

"Share and share alike," said the old guy. "Your feet stink."

"It's a skin infection. I can't help it," spat Fat Gary defensively.

"You'll need to talk to one of the nurses," said Ken. "Not my department to allocate rooms or beds."

"Fuck's sake."

"Do you have any relatives?"

"I'm not from round here." Heavy sarcasm, like it should be obvious from the accent.

"Friends?"

"Those two twats over there are about it." Fat Gary indicated a couple of well-built men with his chins. "Look, how long will I be kept in for?"

"I don't know yet," said Ken, entirely truthfully. "A few more tests and then one of my colleagues will decide."

"The sooner the better. His feet stink!" said the old guy.

"Once I'm up and about, I swear I'll swing for you," Fat Gary threatened.

The old guy just cackled again. Looked like the best fun he'd had in years.

Ken returned the chart, moved to the top of the bed. Shone a torch in each of Fat Gary's eyes as he'd seen on the TV loads of times. Took the opportunity to stick a bug behind the overweight lump's head. Now he'd be able to hear every noise uttered.

"Hmmm," said Ken, sucked in his breath.

"What?" A look of panic swept across Fat Gary's flabby features. His lip quivered like a landed fish.

"I can't say Mr. McSherry. But it's not looking good. You might not have much time left."

"Oh fuck!"

Tears sprang into Fat Gary's eyes. Ken knew he shouldn't have been so childish, but he just hadn't been able to resist. He left the ward, pulled out his mobile as he did so. Texted Frank to tell him he'd tracked down the Scousers. Just a case of waiting now and seeing who turned up.

It didn't take long.

The Thinking Man's Scouser

"I'm looking for a man," said Konstantin.

The woman on front desk duties raised an eyebrow at him. "Aren't we all, love," she said, seventy if she was a day.

"No I meant…"

"Let me handle this," interrupted Fidelity. Outlined what Konstantin had wanted to say, but in a far more eloquent and less provocative fashion.

"Fat and Northern doesn't narrow the field down very much," said the nurse.

"There were three of them, brought in from Broadstairs this morning." Fidelity flashed a bit of cash.

Tip-tap at the keyboard by the old girl and a smile. "Ah yes, here they are."

Fidelity smiled triumphantly at Konstantin. He scowled.

When the slutty woman and huge man were out of sight, the nurse pulled out her mobile. Ignored the commands on posters stuck to every wall that phones should be kept switched off. Sent a quick text to her dealer.

Ken's phone vibrated. He smiled. Forty quid well spent. Positioned himself near the ward entrance and waited.

Watched the pair walk along the corridor. Recognised the big guy instantly. Pretty difficult to forget someone like him. He knew immediately this was going to complicate matters.

First he needed to listen in to what was said. Ken sat down in a communal area with a pair of headphones plugged into his ears.

"This is it," said Fidelity. Pointed at the sign above the double doors. All the wards were named after sunny events. Konstantin wondered whether the person who conceived the idea was being ironic, optimistic or sarcastic.

"Stay here," said Konstantin. Fidelity opened her mouth to argue. He cut her off, said, "Please. For once do as I ask."

"Okay."

Konstantin immediately spotted the guy who'd pointed the gun at him. He was flat out on his back and staring wide eyed at the ceiling, mumbling to himself. He was as pale as his off-white sheets.

"He thinks he's gonna die," said an old guy in the adjacent bed, a huge toothless grin on his face.

"Happens to us all eventually," said Konstantin.

The Russian drew the curtains around Fat Gary's bed, pulled up a chair and sat a foot away from his head. Eventually Fat Gary looked over at Konstantin, recognition sparking in his eyes.

"Hello again," said Konstantin.

"Fuck."

"How are you feeling?"

"I wasn't great to start with, but pretty shit now."

"Why did you try and take me out?"

Fat Gary narrowed his eyes, "You should already know."

"Try me."

"You killed my nephew, Dave."

"Who?"

Fat Gary described Dave the Rave. Good time, drug dealing relative that he used to be.

Konstantin sat back a moment, thought about who he'd met since reaching the UK. Then it clicked. The guy that tried to hustle him the moment Konstantin arrived in Margate.

"I remember him. But it wasn't me who killed him. I didn't even know his name."

"You fucking liar."

"Why would I lie?"

"So you can save your own life."

"Do I look scared to you?"

Fat Gary didn't answer.

"I'll tell you again. I didn't kill Dave. But if you want to come and have another go, feel free. I'll be ready. But next time, bring more men."

Konstantin slipped out the curtains. He found Fidelity sitting on a blue plastic chair fastened to the floor.

"How did it go?" she said.

"Fairly well."

A Bullet For Fatty

Fat Gary thought about his visitor. The big guy had seemed totally certain of himself. It got him thinking. Perhaps someone else had done for Dave after all?

Ken watched Konstantin and his girlfriend depart. Followed them outside to make sure they actually left. Then he rang Frank. Told him who Fat Gary's target had been.

"Bollocks," said Frank.

"I know."

"He did me a favour," said Frank, referring to some trouble with a rogue money lender Konstantin had cleared up.

Ken didn't need to say Frank had been lax in checking out Fat Gary in the first place.

"Uh-huh. What do you want me to do?"

Frank told him.

Fat Gary got dressed behind the curtains. Ignored the banging pain behind his eyelids. He parted the cheap material, glanced through the crack. Saw no one. Both his guys were out of it. They wouldn't be going anywhere fast. But Fat Gary would.

He got lost in the maze of corridors a couple of times before reaching the front desk. Asked some wizened old bitch to get him a taxi fucking pronto. The wrinkly bird pursed her lips but lifted a phone and spoke into it.

Five minutes later he was in the back of a black Mondeo. It smelt clean and fresh. Within moments they were out of Margate and into cabbage strewn fields which didn't. The car pulled off onto a small side road, bumped down a dirt track.

"What's going on?"

"Short cut, mate," said the driver.

The Mondeo stopped by a farm building. It looked derelict. Fat Gary was about to open his mouth to ask another question when the driver turned around, pointed a silenced pistol at his head. Realisation dawned when he recognised the doctor from the hospital.

Which was the last thought that went through Fat Gary's skull before Ken's bullet blew it apart.

Two orderlies entered the ward. They tripped the brakes on a couple of beds and wheeled them out. The Scousers remained unconscious and unaware.

The beds were hustled out a rear entrance, then folded into the back of an ambulance. The orderlies slammed the doors shut before the vehicle drove away.

It wasn't long before Fat Gary's men were beside him in a deep hole. Ken didn't bother to waste a couple of bullets before backfilling it. They'd be dead soon enough.

Payback

The mobile phone did something it hadn't previously. It rang. Konstantin didn't recognise the number, answered anyway.

"Yes?"

"Hello my friend. It's Ken here, from the club. Hopefully you remember me?"

Konstantin did. Said so.

"Good. Just to let you know the little problem with your Northern friends is sorted. You won't be having any more trouble with them."

"Okay."

"Which makes us even for Nikos."

"Fine with me."

"Good. Maybe see you around?"

"Maybe."

Ken ended the call.

"Who was that?" asked Fidelity.

"No one important."

Konstantin thought a moment, said, "You told me you wanted to go on holiday?"

Fidelity smiled. "I know just the place."

Bullet

The Russian Needs Wheels

"I need to borrow your car again," said Konstantin Boryakov. It wasn't a question.

Ken raised an eyebrow, said, "I told you last time we spoke, we're all square. If I loan you a motor, you'll owe me."

"A loan implies rent."

"You're fast, my friend."

"Cash?"

"What else?"

Ken, a small man with hard eyes and far too many tattoos on view, glanced conspiratorially around the nightclub. Konstantin wasn't sure why. Other than a guy behind the bar cleaning glasses, the place was completely empty. He was twenty feet away and seventy if he was a day. Keen hearing probably wasn't one of his abilities.

No surprise, it being the middle of the day. The sound system was silent, the flashing lights hung down, inactive. Only the glitter ball revolved silently, but ultimately completely ineffective.

"Why not buy a car? I know a dealer. Very discreet. I'll make sure you get a good price."

Konstantin shook his head, said, "No records."

"Records can be faked. For a price, of course."

"You going to give me keys or not?"

"Of course. I'm just fucking with you!" Ken smiled a 100 watt beam. Couple of teeth missing. Rotten or punched out Konstantin didn't know. Didn't care. At this rate Ken might lose a few more in the next couple of seconds.

"How much?"

"Fifty a day."

"Steep."

"Beggars can't be choosers. Take it or leave it."

Konstantin recoiled inside momentarily. At first not recognising the euphemism, thinking it an observation instead. The British sense of humour, heavily weighted towards sarcasm, wasn't native to him yet. Probably never would be, but he was having to learn to cope with it.

"Okay." Konstantin stuck out a hand.

Ken eyed the proffered limb like it had six fingers, said, "You want to shake on it? Don't you trust me?"

"No and no. Just want keys."

The other man smiled again. "I wouldn't trust me either. As I said, you're a smart man."

"Not smart, I dealing with you."

Ken laughed this time. Held out his hand, said, "Money first, then the loaner."

Konstantin pulled out a reasonable roll of cash, peeled off £150 in £10 notes.

"You want to be careful flashing that round here. Someone might want to take it," said Ken.

"They welcome to try but dentistry expensive business these days."

"Don't I know it?" Another flash of wasted teeth. "The car is around the back."

They left through a rear fire exit, ended up in a dank, dark, rubbish-strewn alley that smelt of piss.

"Not again," said Konstantin when he laid eyes on a small, brown car that was more rust than metal.

"As I said... beggars and choosers."

"Any guns in boot this time?"

Ken shrugged. "You're asking the wrong guy. Just bring it back in one piece. This is a valuable heirloom. Been in the family for years."

It was Konstantin's turn to raise an eyebrow.

Destination: France (Or Not)

"What the fuck is that?" asked Fidelity Brown, hands on hips, head cocked to one side. Her ruby red lips were puckered into a less than impressed expression. They stood in Konstantin's garage, the bright, tungsten hue from the powerful lights overhead not doing anything positive for the vehicle's appearance.

"Car," said Konstantin.

"It's a shit heap."

"All we have access to."

"I wouldn't be seen dead in it, frankly."

Konstantin shrugged, said, "If you want holiday get in. If not, I see you in couple of days."

"For fuck's sake," said Fidelity, kicked a tyre. Walked around the rust bucket like she was viewing a cow at an auction. One that was on its last legs.

"Your call," pressed Konstantin.

"If I had balls, right now I'd be saying you have them in a sling."

Konstantin frowned. For the second time in the day the manner of speech totally threw him.

"So I go on own or not?"

"No, I'm coming too you fucking idiot."

Konstantin wasn't sure whether to be pleased or not.

Less than an hour later the pair were shuddering at nearly seventy miles an hour on a dual carriageway, like a washing machine on spin. They were near Dover. The road signs said so. No sat nav to hand. Or map book. Two bags in the boot. Neither Konstantin's. They were only going away for a couple of days. Fidelity had struggled to keep the packing lean. Complained bitterly when Konstantin told her to get a move on. And perhaps could she restrict herself to only five pairs of shoes?

"Where next?" said Konstantin.

"Keep going. Straight on."

The rust bucket crawled through the limp port of Dover and out the other side, the road tracking a course above the famous chalk cliffs.

"Tell me when turn off."

"Don't worry, I will."

"I never worry."

The journey continued in silence to Folkestone. First they passed through a large tunnel cut straight through a hill. Once out the other side, the town spread out below the dual carriageway until it met the sea.

"Okay, turn off here," said Fidelity. Then to a busy roundabout. "Straight over."

Konstantin eyed her, said, "This to Eurotunnel." He had to make the turn, already committed.

"Correct."

They were on a back road now, the traffic a lot lighter.

"We going abroad?"

"Uh-huh. I've a hotel booked in Le Touquet. Two rooms of course. No funny business."

The Russian slammed the brakes on, brought the car to a shuddering stop. Elicited an angry blast on a horn from the driver behind. Konstantin looked over his shoulder, glared at the guy. The driver indicated, pulled out and went past the rust bucket at a sedate pace. He kept his eyes averted, like if he didn't see Konstantin he wasn't there.

"What's the matter?" asked Fidelity. Anger flared in her eyes. "Were you expecting us to be in the same bed? Because you can fucking forget it!"

"I can't go."

"Why?"

"No passport."

"What? Everyone has a passport!"

"Not me."

"Then how did you get to England?"

"Long story, now not time. Let's just say I not popular with authorities."

"Oh." Fidelity looked totally deflated, like she had no idea what to do next. Her anger burnt out.

Konstantin put the car back in gear, drove on. Headed back to the motorway. Kept driving, no idea where to go, but continued away from Margate and deeper into Kent.

After several miles of silence Fidelity finally spoke, said, "I was just trying to do something nice. Have an adventure."

"I know."

"I'm sorry I accused you of…"

Konstantin shrugged.

"It's been a long time since I did anything exciting," said Fidelity.

"I sick of exciting. Quiet is cool."

Fidelity fell silent again. Konstantin saw an exit ahead, decided he'd take it and turn around, go back to where he lived.

As he kicked on the indicator, Fidelity's head snapped up. Looked around, sudden recognition in her eyes. She leant over. Turned off the indicator.

"Keep going," she said.

"Where to?"

Fidelity eventually whispered, "Dungeness."

"Where?"

Then, so quietly he almost missed it, she said, "Home."

Isolated Splendour

The sky was darkening to a slate grey by the time Konstantin steered the rust bucket into the small seaside town. Not that the Russian could truly gauge its size. The lack of light and the foul weather made visibility extremely limited.

A torrent of rain slashed across the windscreen. So hard the wipers were struggling to keep up. As if the car was under a waterfall or undergoing a particularly violent car wash.

It felt like civilisation was a long way behind them. Buildings had given way to wide open spaces. The roads narrowed, the lighting less frequent. Then huge pylons dominated the skyline, marching like soldiers across the landscape, all leading to a rectangular block of illumination on the horizon. Fidelity had told Konstantin the cubist rendering was actually a redundant nuclear power station.

The landscape was almost totally flat. Other than the detritus linked to the power station and the occasional leaning tree, there were no visible landmarks. So nothing to deter the wind – and it roared, buffeted the car with an unseen hand.

Konstantin leant over the steering wheel, getting as close to the windscreen as possible, as if watching a television with a poor picture. He rubbed a sleeve at the glass, smearing away the condensation. The air conditioning wasn't operating. No amount of twisting of knobs on the dashboard coaxed the slightest of draughts from the vents.

"How far?" asked Konstantin. The car rocked with another gust of wind.

"We're near."

"Good."

Then there was the twinkle of lights on the horizon. A single, weak strand that stretched left to right.

"This is it."

"Okay."

The road remained narrow, barely lit. Konstantin drove slowly, not wanting to end up in a ditch. Then night went totally black. The streetlights cut out, the houses too. Only the headlamps cut through the gloom. Stretched about ten raindrops out.

"Power cut," explained Fidelity. "Used to happen a lot when I lived around here. Looks like it still does."

The rust bucket took them into a village, a couple of roads and a jumble of houses arranged either side. Konstantin slowed to walking pace, halted at a junction. The road curved left and right. The engine idled, although he couldn't hear it over the howling wind.

"Where we heading?"

"My aunt's house," said Fidelity and pointed.

Konstantin forced the car into gear, elicited some grinding noises. Twisted the wheel right as far as it would go. The rust bucket swung in a narrow arc onto a single track road. In seconds, the habitation gone.

"Stop," said Fidelity after a minute's crawl. Konstantin couldn't see any distinguishing feature and told her so.

"You get used to finding your way around in the dark here," she shrugged.

He parked as close to the building as possible. The headlights picked out a section of dark stone, the rest almost invisible in the shitty weather.

"Ready?" asked Fidelity.

Konstantin nodded.

Fidelity pushed hard on the door, immediately the blast of wind and rain entered, soaking her and the interior. She slammed the door then ran, head down, towards the house. Konstantin did the same, slightly more protected from the foul weather by the car body. Nevertheless, he was soaked through in seconds. He didn't bother to lock up.

The pair stood in the porch, dripping like drowned kittens. A pool formed at Konstantin's feet. Outside the wind tugged at the thin door and roof, trying to rip both away.

Fidelity pushed her hair out of her eyes, knocked on the door, waited.

Nothing.

She rapped again, louder this time. The sound echoed through the house.

"Oh. Looks like she isn't in."

"Who?"

"My aunt Kathy."

"Now what?"

"I guess we've two choices – car or porch?"

"What about the pub?"

Konstantin couldn't see Fidelity's face, but he could hear the tension in her voice. "No."

"Car."

"Shit. I thought you'd say that."

"Ready?"

Morning Glory

Something was tapping the inside of his skull. A pause, then resumed. Louder. More urgent.

Konstantin cracked open one eye, glanced around. Saw brightness and not a lot else. Then the outline of a person at the window. A woman came into view, revealed by opening both eyes. Grey hair tied up, lines on her face. Weathered would be the best description. Like a hard wood.

Konstantin sat up, heard and felt something crack in his spine. He wound the window down. It took a while.

"Can I help you?" said the woman. She looked past Konstantin at Fidelity who was curled up on the flattened out passenger seat in a foetal position.

"We're okay thanks." Konstantin dropped into English, lost the Russian inflection.

"It's just that you're parked in my front garden," she said.

He looked out, couldn't see any obvious demarcation from beach to house.

"Sorry."

"Who's your friend?"

Konstantin leant over, shook Fidelity's shoulder gently. She shot bolt upright, her eyes wild, ready to fight or flee.

"Fidelity? Is that you?"

"Thanks Auntie Kathy," said Fidelity. Blew across the cup of coffee she'd just been handed.

"You two should get a shower," said Kathy.

"I don't think your Aunt meant together," said Konstantin, interpreting the look of shock on Fidelity's face.

"No, I certainly didn't!"

Fidelity laughed. Sounded a little forced.

They were seated in a conservatory at the rear of Kathy's small house. It looked out to the sea, a brown smear under a bruised sky. The beach was a huge expanse of flint rocks and pebbles. Both seemed to go on forever. Konstantin couldn't help staring.

"Impressive, isn't it?" asked Kathy.

Konstantin nodded, said, "How long have you lived here?"

"My whole life. I couldn't imagine being anywhere else. I love it."

The Russian could see why. He itched to get out and about, to really explore this alien landscape. Konstantin looked from Fidelity to Kathy and back again. The pair was avoiding each other's eyes. He suddenly felt like a stupid male of the species, totally impervious to the subliminal signals being sent between them, too busy admiring the view to notice.

"If you don't mind, I'll go out for a walk," he said.

"Don't feel you have to," said Kathy, but sounded like she didn't mean a syllable.

"No, I'd like to."

"There's a raincoat hanging up in the porch. Just in case it comes down again."

Konstantin nodded. Walked through the house, out the front door. Ignored the coat. Didn't mind if he got wet again. Quite liked it really. He was just glad not to be inside.

Took a moment to look around. Behind loomed the massive power station, away from which snaked a multitude of power cables and pylons. To the front was the sea and sky. Left, the small village and right a strange jumble of outbuildings spread over a wide area.

He decided to walk straight forward. The flints scrunched and scraped underfoot, sounding more like metal than stone. Soon the bank dropped away, indicating the high tide mark. A steep incline and he was on sand. The tide was way out, at least a mile across the flats. When the water decided to return it would do so quickly. He sat down, invisible to everything and everyone. The first time he'd chosen to do so for as long as he could remember.

Secrets and Lies

"You got my letter then?" said Kathy eventually. She looked over the top of her mug at Fidelity. She wouldn't meet her aunt's eyes. Simply stared at the huge sky.

"No."

Kathy crossed her brows, said, "I sent it to the address you gave me."

"I moved."

"When?"

"Can't remember."

"Why didn't you let me know where you'd gone?"

A shrug from Fidelity did little to lift Kathy's mood. She decided a metaphoric slap might work.

"Then you won't know your brother is back."

Fidelity's head flicked around, her eyes wide. "He's here?"

"Yes."

Fidelity stood and went to the French windows, craned her head left and right.

"Where?"

"His old place. But as usual he spends most of his waking time at The Pilot."

So only a few hundred yards away then, Fidelity realised. She could be there in moments, stretching her fingers around his scrawny neck. Choking the life out of the bastard...

"Has he been to see you?"

"Not so far," Kathy lied.

"Thank fuck."

"He knows what would happen if he did."

"Thanks."

Kathy felt a wave of guilt, but stamped on it. A gust of wind rattled the conservatory, momentarily breaking the conversation.

"If you're not here for George, why are you?" asked Kathy.

"I honestly don't know. Chance really."

"How long will you stay for?"

"I'm reconsidering my options right now. Days, before. Now? Minutes, maybe."

"That's a shame."

"But you can't really blame me, can you?"

"I suppose not, under the circumstances. And what about your friend? Does he know anything?"

"No. Not yet. And for now I'd like to keep it that way."

"You like him." For once it wasn't a question emerging from Kathy's mouth.

"No."

"It's okay to, you know."

"I don't know what I think. But it's not important."

"It's a hell of a secret to keep," said Kathy.

The younger woman shrugged. "I've managed so far."

"Maybe it's time for it to come out. Maybe that's why you're here, my girl."

Fidelity didn't answer, stayed staring out to sea. Eyes on nothing. Heard Kathy leave the room.

Tears pricked at Fidelity's eyes. She brushed them away angrily. Hadn't cried for ages, wasn't going to now. Never again.

She thought about her secret and the Russian.

It's not whether he likes me or not.

If he knew everything, there'd be only one opinion he could possibly hold about me.

Slut.

Dog Days

He felt like one of those Antony Gormley statues. Upright, unmoving, staring out to sea. The Dover coastline, with its iconic white cliffs, was just to his left. Other than that it was air, light and water. Truly elemental.

Konstantin hadn't managed to sit still for more than a few minutes. Now he was all the way out to where the surf broke in gentle waves. Stood a few minutes, absently watched the tide. Noticed it was on the turn, began lapping at his toes. Decided he would turn as well. Reversed direction and walked quickly back over the shiny sand.

Hit the stones, saw the cottage. Fidelity at the window, staring out. Whether at him, he wasn't sure. Maybe now wasn't the time to go back.

Shoulders hunched against the wind, the Russian decided to investigate the village, now he could see it. Frankly, the impression wasn't much different to the first gained last night. Houses centred around a pub. A couple of roads, a couple of shops. Mostly selling fish. Then a line of more modern residences stretching away in the distance. They'd be the ones he'd seen last night, before the power went out.

Decided to hit the place where everything happened in a small town. The local drinking establishment. Here, it was called The Pilot. Right on the beach. A decent car park, white weatherboarded building. Low, spread out. A good idea here. Dealt with the weather better. The few trees and shrubs he'd seen were the same. The branches furled in one direction – that of the wind.

The interior was well laid out. Bar with hand pumps and optics, tables, chairs. Dartboard and pool table. Menu on the wall showing they did food as well as alcohol. High in calories, low in cost.

The residents clearly weren't bothered by people from out of town. No pause in speech as he entered. The buzz of conversation, the clink of glasses continued unabated. Only a dog made its discomfort known. Lifted its head, growled. Konstantin didn't know the breed, hadn't ever owned a pet.

His only contact in the past had been trained attack dogs. Those he avoided, or killed if he couldn't. Too many sharp teeth, too little compassion. The owner, sat at the bar nursing a pint, yanked on its lead. Told the animal to shut the fuck up.

Konstantin reached the bar, rested his hands on top, leaned in to get some attention from the staff. The dog owner drained his pint, raised it and waved the glass with the same aim in mind. A young girl walked over, stopped in front of Konstantin.

"What can I get you?" she said. Tall, skinny, hair pulled back in an untidy pile on top of her skull. Picked up a whiff of stale cigarettes. Konstantin could see a couple of tattoos and piercings. Fashionable, then.

"I was next, Katrina," said the dog owner.

She turned her eyes onto him, said, "No you're not. This man was here first. You were still drinking as he arrived."

"You're wrong." He slammed his palm down on the bar. Sounded like a slap across her face. "Get me. A fucking. Pint."

The pub fell silent. Konstantin could feel dozens of eyes swivel onto the action.

Katrina remained utterly impassive, repeated her question of Konstantin. For a moment he considered giving ground to the guy, allowing the other's childishness to win, but knew it would be weak to do so.

"Vodka."

"Single or double?"

"Double. No ice."

"For fuck's sake, you're serving him before a local?" the man asked, tone tinged with incredulity.

"Looks like it," said Katrina as she exercised an optic. The clear liquid drained into the small glass the barmaid held. "Anyway, strictly you're not a local these days."

"Good job for you I don't punch bitches."

Konstantin saw the guy slide off his stool as Katrina placed Konstantin's drink on the bar. Watched him in his peripheral vision. He turned ninety degrees, stood inches away from Konstantin, who ignored him. He could feel his presence, an alarm bell ringing. The dog growled again.

"Well I think that's shit."

"Nobody cares what you *think*, George," said Katrina.

Konstantin threw the glass back, felt the spirit drain down his throat. Warmed him from the inside, first time in twenty four hours.

"Another please," said Konstantin.

George put his arm out, right across Konstantin. Blocked him from the bar.

"It's my fucking turn to get a drink."

Now the Russian swivelled to face George, properly looked at him. Towered over the man, but then he did over most people. He was tanned, incredibly wiry. The tendons on his neck stood out like cords. A heavy lifter. Wasn't wearing much, shorts and a shirt. As if he was used to working outside in all weathers. Postmen, they were the same. Some sort of macho thing to don minimal gear, whatever the climate.

But George didn't step down. Came in even closer, eyes below Konstantin's chin.

"Go on granddad. Take a swing," he said. The dog's growl went up a notch.

"Back off, George," said Katrina.

"Stay out of this," he replied, not taking his eyes off Konstantin.

"I'll have no fighting in here."

"He's asked for it."

"No, he asked for a drink."

"Come on, hit me!" shouted George, spit flying, teeth bared like the dog.

Konstantin noted George kept his left hand out of sight. More than likely a concealed weapon. Knife, screwdriver with a sharpened tip. Something like that. Would bet he'd done jail time and a shank would be like a limb. Essential and never left in his cell.

"I'll bar you unless you stop this now," said Katrina. "I mean it!"

"You can't bar me, I live here."

"Then that'll be a big problem for you, won't it?"

Konstantin decided to take matters into his own hands, literally. In a blur, he punched out with his left fist and blocked with his right. The former struck George hard in his bollocks, the latter to counter any strike with the weapon. George groaned deeply, bent over double, collapsed to the floor. A screwdriver skittered across the floorboards.

Katrina looked at him, asked, "Was that really necessary?"

Konstantin picked up the makeshift weapon, placed it on the bar along with a five pound note. "Yes."

Turned and left before he picked up a ban. Didn't wait for the change.

A Kick in the Nuts

Kathy hadn't enjoyed lying to Fidelity, but felt she'd needed to. George had been to her house. The second thing the bastard had done when he'd returned 'home'.

George had hammered on the door until she answered. It took her a moment to recognise him. He'd changed so much. Thinner and harder in the face, hair cut to the scalp, unshaven. Kathy could smell the body odour out of his armpits, the alcohol seeping out of his pores, revealing his first activity – going to the pub.

She tried to slam the door shut then, but too late. George had his foot in the way. Pushed the door open, Kathy didn't resist. Couldn't anyway. He was too powerful.

"Is she here?"

"Who?"

"You fucking know who," he slurred. "My bitch of a sister."

Kathy sighed. Didn't like the language. Not the swearing, the words directed at Fidelity.

"No. She's not, George."

"You'd better not be lying. You know how much I loathe bullshitters."

She said nothing, just glared at him. Eventually said, "Get out of here and leave me alone."

George looked her up and down then. "I hadn't realised."

"What?"

"You're not bad for an older woman. But then again, I am pissed."

Kathy stamped down hard on George's foot. He yelled, jerked it backwards. She slammed the door shut, locked it before he could react, leant against it. Felt and heard George thump on the wood several times, call her a bitch, and worse. She closed her eyes, wished he'd go away.

After a minute her desire was fulfilled. Another kick, another 'bitch' and he was gone. Kathy let out a huge sigh. Decided there and then she needed to write to Fidelity. Warn her.

Pity it hadn't worked.

Once George Parker had picked himself off the floor, he flopped down in a chair for five minutes and let the pain in his mid-region subside. He noted that no one offered him a helping hand. Well, the lot of them could just fuck right off.

He tried to stand, ended back on his arse again. His bollocks just hurt too much. On the second attempt he just about managed it. Limped across the bar. Stared at the regulars as he passed them. None met his gaze. If any had done so they'd have received a mouthful for sure. Either words or knuckles. Maybe both.

Ironically the public phone was in a corner by the public toilets. George could smell the urine and disinfectant as he fed the slot with coins. Tapped in a number from memory. Took a while for it to be picked up.

When he'd finished George replaced the receiver, grinned himself a nasty grin. Returned to the bar. His dog, a German Shepherd called Mutt, was lying on the floor, taking up a vast amount of space.

"Do you still want that pint?" asked Katrina. George was about to unhook the lead, changed his mind.

"Yeah, why not," he said. Took less time to drain the glass than fill it. Tossed a fiver at Katrina, told her to keep the change.

"You owe me £7.40."

He scooped up the blue note. Replaced with a brown one. Grabbed the dog's lead, yanked on it. The beast jerked to its feet.

Outside, George swung a leg over the seat of his motorbike. A Royal Enfield Bullet. Seen better days, black paint and chrome slightly shabby, but it had a modified 500cc engine. Plenty of power, attested to by the roar of compressed gas out the exhausts when George kicked it into life.

He slotted the lead over the handlebar and pulled out of the car park. The dog trotted beside him, tongue lolling. Left town and headed along the coast at a sedate pace.

Eventually reached a ramshackle building, more shack than shed. It stood by itself on the wrong side of the road. Near the sea. Got the full force of the weather. Which is why it had been empty and the owner happy to lease it. Cheaply and for cash. Left the bike and the dog outside. Entered. It comprised two indistinct spaces – living room and bedroom. He went into the latter, lay down.

After only a few minutes he rose again, retraced his route. His blood was up.

Fidelity's Puzzle

Katrina stepped outside about half an hour later. She leaned against the wall, raised her right leg and flattened the sole onto the weatherboard in a flamingo pose. Inserted a fag between her ruby lips, a small ring through the lower one Konstantin hadn't noticed before.

Spark of a lighter, a yellow flame. The tip burned as the barmaid sucked in. Rested her head back. She held the smoke in for long moments, hissed it out through her teeth.

"Better?" asked Konstantin.

Katrina didn't react. Nerves of steel this one. Eventually shrugged.

"What do you want?"

He seemed to be getting that question a lot today.

"George, who is he?"

The barmaid sucked in another lungful of airborne nicotine, ejected it via her nose this time. Obviously a natural talent for smoking.

"Bad news."

"Clearly."

"Why are you interested?"

"Because I'm in town for a couple of days. It's a small place. I want to know if more trouble is coming."

Katrina laughed. It wasn't a pleasant sound. "You can bet on it. You embarrassed him in public. George Parker is an eye for an eye kind of guy."

"So I'll be seeing him again."

"It's a racing certainty."

"Good," said Konstantin.

"What did he do?"

Katrina looked at him for the first time. "Run that by me again."

"What's his story?"

"Nothing really. Just the local trouble maker. Likes a drink, prefers a fight. I was at school with him. Same class. It wasn't fun."

"Sounds like a nice guy."

"He's all heart."

"I'll leave you to the rest of your cancer stick."

"Yeah, yeah. Heard it all before."

There wasn't anywhere else to go, so Konstantin headed back to Kathy's. Didn't take long. Stuck to the roads this time. Saved a few seconds in transit time. But the vista wasn't as agreeable.

Didn't knock, twisted the handle and stepped inside. Stood still for a moment, listened. Could hear the sound of running water. A shower, most likely.

Konstantin entered the kitchen, searched the cupboards for some coffee. Sighed when he only found instant. Decided he'd rather dehydrate or drink gravy.

"We brought the bags in," said Kathy.

He hadn't heard her arrival and was quite impressed.

"Thanks."

"You can get a shower once Fidelity is out. There should be plenty of water. In the meantime I'll cook us some lunch."

"Okay."

"Would you mind?" asked Kathy. The kitchen was small, a tight fit for two normal sized people, never mind one of them being Konstantin.

"Sorry." The Russian shuffled out of the way, allowed Kathy to the cooker. She busied herself with pots and pans, kept her back turned.

"I met someone earlier," said Konstantin.

"Oh?" Didn't sound interested.

"George Parker. Do you know him?"

Kathy froze for a moment, squeezed out, "Who?"

"I think you heard my question."

"Sorry, he's not familiar to me."

"He grew up around here. The girl in the pub told me so. This place is small, everyone knows everyone."

"Why are you interested?"

"That's the second time I've had that said to me today. I had some trouble with him earlier. Please, just tell me the truth."

A large sigh emanated from Kathy. She turned, propped herself up at the cooker. "I know George. I just wish I didn't."

Konstantin kept quiet, let the moment stretch. Sometimes it was better to say nothing.

"He's Fidelity's brother. Well, half-brother really. Different fathers. Different people in every respect as you've probably noticed."

"They're both strong characters."

"True."

"What else?"

"He's a trouble causer, always has been. Thieving, fighting. Went with a bad crowd. He was a one man crimewave. Then one day he just upped and disappeared. No warning. He was here one minute, gone the next. That was a good day."

"Why?"

Kathy shrugged. "No idea and I didn't care."

"How long was he gone for?"

"Two years. I'd all but forgotten about him until he showed his face last week."

"Where had he been?"

"Also no idea. I haven't asked him and frankly, I couldn't give a shit. Now, can you let me cook lunch?"

Kathy turned away, presented the Russian with her back again. Conversation over. Silence, just the ticking of a clock somewhere.

"Sounds like the shower's free," she said.

Dismissed, Konstantin left the room. Passed Fidelity on the stairs. She was furiously towelling her hair dry. Another towel, which looked far too small for the job, was wrapped around her midriff. She winked, gave him a little smile. Konstantin forced the ghost of a response.

He knew. So did Kathy. She wasn't lying. Just wasn't telling the whole truth. Nothing like the whole truth and so help me God. Konstantin wondered why. Went into the bathroom, turned the shower onto cold. Stepped underneath the soft stream. Deliberated how Fidelity was connected.

But Konstantin spent far more time trying to understand why he cared.

Peeping George

George was outside when the big guy went inside. Didn't need the binoculars around his neck to see the oversized bastard. That he entered Kathy's house without knocking inferred familiarity. Which was odd, as George had never clapped eyes on him until today. Then again he'd only been back in Dungeness a week.

What was he? A lover? Maybe Kathy had fallen on hard times and was taking lodgers? Or she was running a B&B now? Unlikely though, the woman was staunchly protective of her independence. George should know, he'd offered her his companionship on many an occasion.

Of course the woman had taken offence. Told him to fuck off every time. Said she was a lesbian, although that seemed to be another lie, looking at the evidence before him.

Women, they were all the same. Like that Katrina in the pub. Manipulative. Liars. Self-interested. Never met one he could trust. They took what they wanted from an honest, hard-working man like him and squeezed until you were dry. Then discarded you and moved onto the next sucker. It had happened his whole life. Even his mother had walked out on him.

That's why he'd left, more than two years ago now. To get away from all of them.

George put the binoculars back to his eyes. Nearly fell over when he saw the face in the lens. The worst of them all.

Fidelity.

That changed the plan somewhat.

White Van Men

It was late afternoon by the time a knackered transit van, belching smoke from a straw sized exhaust, rattled through Dungeness. The mud spattered vehicle pulled into the pub car park, across two bays. The engine knocked when it was turned off. The doors opened.

Out stepped two men. One went to the rear, flung up the roller. Two more men leapt down. Eyes scanned the immediate environment. Didn't take long.

Hard men, tough men who'd lived on the wrong side of life. Still did. Fags were immediately lit.

"Where the fuck is he?"

"He said he'd be here, he'll be here." Yorkshire accent.

"I hate this place."

"Why?"

"It smells clean. Fresh, like."

They heard the bike in the distance. Fell silent. The tone grew in strength as it neared. Throaty, powerful. George swung into the car park. Stopped the Bullet adjacent to the transit.

Shook their hands one by one. Palms rough to the touch. Sandpaper on sandpaper. Lit up too. Looked at the guys as he smoked. Like something out of a circus freak show.

Bob. Pot-bellied. Bald. The self-appointed leader.

Glenn. Short stature. Short fuse. Punchy.

Craig. Mr. tattoo. Ginger hair. Barely ever spoke.

Shaun. Lazy eye. Gimpy leg. Lisp.

"You made it," said George.

"'Course, told you we would. Middle of fucking nowhere though, ain't it?" Bob replied.

"We've lived in worse."

"True, mate. But I prefer a bit of noise. Here it's… quiet." Bob dumped his fag. "So, you said something about a spot of bother that needed sorting?"

"Yep," replied George. "How about talking over a pint?"

"Best fucking idea I've heard all day. My throat's as dry as a nun's chuff. Alright lads?"

Got three nods in response.

George led them inside the pub. Settled the guys at a table. Bought five pints he could ill afford from the bitch Katrina. Hated the idea of lining the woman's pocket.

"Going to bring them over?" he asked.

"No," she said. "Too busy."

George looked around, saw only a couple of other people in the place. He growled when she raised an eyebrow at him, decided he'd wipe the smirk off her face later. In a way Katrina wouldn't enjoy. At first anyway. She passed a tray over. He transferred the glasses from bar to tray, carried them the short distance.

"Fuck's sake, you've spilled most of it!" grumbled Shaun.

George shrugged, said, "Free ain't it, you tight fisted bastard?"

He sat down, got stuck with the stool when everyone else had chairs.

"You call this dump home?" said Bob loudly. Got a few looks from the regulars.

"It was, hasn't been for a long time. Just somewhere I stayed 'til I could move on."

"What's there to do here? Any more pubs?"

"Fishing, sailing mainly. And no, this is the only one."

"Fuck's sake."

"Lager's ok though."

"Yeah, I guess it'll do the job."

"Talking about jobs…," said George.

Bob held his hand up, said, "Hold your fucking horses. We want a few drinks first. Thirsty work all that driving."

"Strictly it wasn't you that did the driving," said Glenn. "It was Craig what did."

Bob shrugged, said, "So?"

"I was just saying, is all," grumbled Glenn, all surly as was his way.

"Well don't. Take a leaf out of Craig's book and shut the fuck up."

The group fell silent. George was used to this lot speaking very little, particularly when Bob started throwing his ample weight around. But mostly it was because they all had grim life stories and therefore plenty of bile within. No -one wanted to discuss why they'd ended up in a dead-end, shit strewn alley of life. Particularly George. Most days the silence suited him. Although not right now. He was bursting with information, felt compelled to spill his guts.

But on the other hand he knew the boys wouldn't like it, would feel repelled by his outpouring. Bob, of course, more than any other. He'd the worst background from what George pieced together from snippets – words which slipped out when roaring drunk. Guard momentarily down.

So George stayed quiet for now.

"Get us another in," said Bob, waved his drained glass in front of George before placing it on the sodden tray.

Four more joined.

"What? I'm not made of money you know."

Bob leaned into George's face. Revealed the tattoos on his neck. The stale breath. Coffee, burger, nicotine.

"Four hours driving to get here. And we spent thirty five quid on petrol. Another thirty five to get back again. Plus we're not working. So, least you can do is buy your mates a fucking lager."

Briefly, George wondered whether he'd made a mistake bringing Bob and the boys down. Too late remembering they weren't friends, couldn't possibly be. Were just people with a shared situation.

But the die was cast.

George went to the bar.

Give Us A Pint

Katrina made sure the idiots with George were piled high with alcohol and crisps.

"Need anything else?" she asked, waved her packet of fags at them.

"Nah, off you go love," said the one she'd heard called Bob.

Slipped out the back, but didn't light up. Instead, ran to Kathy's house.

When she returned George was at the bar again with a stack of empty glasses, tapping his fingers on the varnished wood.

"You look out of breath, love. Should give them fags up."

"Yeah, you're probably right. More lager?" Katrina asked.

"How did you guess? Hope the barrels are full."

"No need to worry about it. We've plenty."

"It takes a lot to bother me, love." George winked.

Katrina shrugged, got to pulling the pints.

Playing Statues

"Who was that at the door?" shouted Kathy from the living room.

"Jehovah's Witness," replied Konstantin as he walked back in. Saw the puzzled look on her face.

"Well that's a first," she said.

"They get everywhere," he shrugged. "I need a walk. Anyone joining me?"

Fidelity looked out the window, took in the fast blackening skies, the increasing wind and the threat of rain.

"You're kidding, right?" she said.

"No. It's good exercise," said Konstantin.

"You're okay. I think we'll be staying here," said Fidelity, just as Konstantin expected.

He heard an incredulous laugh erupt from her as he closed the door and smiled to himself.

Konstantin headed onto the beach, drifted into the dark. He wouldn't be seen from ten feet away. But he could see ashore because of the street lighting.

Walked a few hundred yards. Wasn't concerned about the noise, the tide was in and the crashing of the waves was cacophonous. He enjoyed the rhythmic pulse of the water, the rush as it pulled back through the stones. Like the strangled breathing of some huge sea beast.

Before long, the white weatherboard of the pub was clearly visible. Spotlights marked it out. Konstantin entered the car park, checked out the van he knew the men had arrived in. The doors were unlocked.

Nothing of note inside other than a bag of weed, four sleeping bags and a powerful odour that was the opposite of pleasant.

He took a moment to look over the motorbike standing a few feet away. A Royal Enfield Bullet apparently. Seemed relatively ordinary. Bit rusty, ragged around the edges but had chunky exhausts. Maybe it had hidden depths.

The Russian faded back into the gloom, stood with the sea at his rear, watched the door. He was used to remaining motionless in one position. If it took a couple of hours, he didn't mind. Suspected they wouldn't roll out until closing time.

Which was a couple of hours away.

Konstantin was ultimately proved correct.

Smiled as he watched Katrina manhandle the men out of her pub, one after the other. Five of them. Quite impressive. He only recognised George, the others utterly unfamiliar. From Katrina's description the fat guy would be Bob, the leader.

There was a lot of swearing, all directed at the barmaid. She gave them the finger, slammed the door closed. Locked it.

After some debate three of the gang fell into the van, shut the door. George, then Bob managed to mount the motorbike. Took several kicks to get the engine going. It emitted a powerful rumble, Konstantin appreciated the sound. Definitely hidden depths. George revved it a couple of times then steered the Bullet out of the car park. He listened to it retreat up the road, picked up a couple of gear changes. Eventually the noise died away. Left just the wind and waves. The van rocked as the minions inside adjusted their positions, then lay still.

Konstantin remained on the beach for another hour. Let them acquire a solid state of unconsciousness.

Eventually decided the time was right and walked off the beach. Slowly opened the driver's door, stuffed George's screwdriver into the ignition. Started the engine, pulled away sedately. Drove like the van was a hearse. Fearful of disturbing the dead.

Konstantin drove the van for about two miles, deep into the countryside. Found a derelict building, an old barn. Roof coming down, doors long gone. He reversed in until the cab met the wall, literally. Turned the engine off. Bent down, pulled the plastic cowling off from under the steering wheel. Tore the wires out so it couldn't be started even if the guys managed to get out.

Started the hike back to Dungeness. It wasn't far to run.

He was barely out of breath by the time Konstantin arrived back at Kathy's. He was pleased with his evening's work. Had shortened the odds dramatically.

Crept up the stairs, tried to keep the noise to a minimum. Entered his bedroom and closed the door silently behind him. Blinked in surprise when the bedside lamp was flicked on.

Fidelity sat on his bed, said, "I need to tell you something."

"No. You don't."

"I have to. Please sit with me."

Konstantin, after a moment's pause, took off his jacket and laid it on a chair. Lowered himself onto the bed. Kicked his shoes off. Swivelled around. Put his back against the headrest. Shiny, twisted brass. Uncomfortable, but he barely noticed. Fidelity shuffled up to him. She had to. It was a single and she'd be on the floor otherwise. Konstantin almost jerked at the touch of her body.

She leant over, clicked off the light. Began to recount her dark history.

Dawn was nearing. Fidelity slept. Exhausted because of her emotional outpouring. Konstantin, however, was wide awake. Thinking.

Eventually he rose carefully. Fidelity remained unconscious. He pulled a cover over her. Picked up his shoes and jacket. Crept back down the stairs. Left the house and walked to the pub. Saw a fishing boat out to sea, a smattering of seagulls following the wake. No one else around. Which wasn't a surprise.

He banged on the door until Katrina opened it. Hair everywhere, she looked less than impressed.

"This had better be important," she said.

"If George comes in today call me immediately please." Konstantin passed over a piece of paper with eleven numbers on. She glanced at it. Shoved the note into her dressing gown pocket.

"Sure."

"Thanks."

"Can I go back to bed now?"

"Yes. Sorry."

"Don't mention it. But don't make it a habit either."

Konstantin made himself a coffee. Instant. He needed it. Couldn't quite ignore the dried shit taste. Dumped in some milk to tone it down.

Went into the conservatory, sat down facing the sea view.

"Couldn't sleep either?" asked Kathy. Like Katrina she was in a dressing gown, although she had bunny slippers on her feet.

"No. Too much on my mind."

"My conscience is clear," she said. "I just don't like to waste my days any more. I'm not sure how many I've left."

"You're not old."

"That's kind to say, but I'm not taking any chances."

Konstantin looked out to sea. Kathy took the other seat, said, "She told you then?"

"Yes."

Kathy sighed. "That was very brave of her."

"Yes."

"What are you planning to do?"

"Do you have a boat?"

"Almost everyone here does."

"May I borrow it?"

"Only if you'll be up to no good."

"Promise," Konstantin said. "Hope to die."

The Boys Are Missing

"What the fuck?" managed Bob. He couldn't believe his eyes. The car park was bereft of vans, but there were plenty of cars. Lunch time and the pub was doing a decent trade by the looks of it. "Where are they?"

George shrugged. Didn't care right now. Had King Kong's hangover. Delivered a murderous glare to a seagull who dared to squawk in his general direction. The bird didn't care. Did it again. George gathered up a stone. Chucked it at the winged rat. It took to the air, unfazed by its treatment.

"Give them a call," he suggested. Leant against the Bullet. Took the weight off his head.

Bob grunted, like he should have thought of that himself. Pulled a mobile out of his pocket. Tapped in a number, listened while it rang.

"Fuck's sake," said Bob.

"No answer?"

"You think?"

George let the sarcasm pass him by. He felt too rough to react to it. Bob tried again.

On the fifth occasion someone must have answered as Bob said, "About time!"

George could only hear the one side of the conversation, which went:

"Glenn you tosser, where are you?"

"I know you're in the van, you idiot, but where's the van?"

"'Here' doesn't give me much of a clue. Try again."

"Well I'm in the car park. You're not, which is why I'm ringing you."

"Yes I am fucking sure!"

"I can't be bothered with this shite."

Bob took the phone away from his ear, growled at the heavens, disconnected the call.

"Well?" asked George.

"Well what?"

"Where are they?"

George thought Bob was going to explode. His face went beetroot red in an instant. Ground his teeth, clenched and unclenched his fists. Heaved huge gusts of breath.

"I don't know," he eventually said. "They don't know."

"Oh."

"I need a pint. You're buying."

Katrina was behind the bar again. She rolled her eyes when George and Bob entered, said, "What do you want?"

"That's no way to treat paying customers," said Bob, oozing misplaced charm.

"If you remember, I chucked you out last night for trying to grab my arse."

"Did I? Sorry about that," Bob said, a huge grin betraying his lack of remorse. "How about I buy you a drink to make up for it?"

"How about 'fuck off'?"

Bob laughed, said, "Your loss, love."

"Hardly. Look, I've people to serve. Make a choice or go away."

"Pint of lager and one of your cheese sarnies. He's paying." Bob crooked a thumb at George, who shook his head in irritation.

Katrina dialled the number, waited for it to connect. Kept her voice down, even though she was in the back room well away from the bar. Told Konstantin who was throwing down the beer.

Went back to the hubbub. Shouted at everyone to drink up and get the fuck out.

And Bob Wanted To Puke

His bulk blocked the doorway. Shadow stretched long into the now dimly lit pub. Proved he wasn't a vampire. Konstantin glanced around, saw George and Bob resolutely seated at a table. Refused to go until they'd finished their pints. They were the last remaining patrons.

Katrina stood behind the bar, arms crossed, fingers tapping on bicep. Konstantin remembered her question. "You're not going to smash the place up are you?"

He'd said no. Which hadn't entirely been a lie because it would probably be George's face doing the smashing.

Konstantin nodded at her and she reluctantly departed. George looked over his shoulder, obviously clocked that she was in on it when he said, "I'll be coming for you once I've finished with him."

The Russian closed the door. Slid the bolts across. Top and bottom. No one else in. No one else out. He crossed the room, weaving between the tables. Konstantin's head pounded. Still hadn't driven the fury away. Reached the pair, glared from one to the other. Bob couldn't hold his gaze. Glanced away, put the glass to his lips and drained the remaining lager.

"I think I'll be going," he said.

"No," said Konstantin. Pulled out a stool, sat down opposite. "You need to hear this."

"Hear what?" asked George.

"You know."

He shrugged. Sneered. Reached out to take a crisp from the packet on the table. Konstantin struck like a snake. Stabbed George's own screwdriver through the back of his hand. The sharpened tip slid easily through skin and bit deeply into the wood.

George shrieked. The colour drained out of his face as if someone had pulled a plug. He tried to tug the screwdriver out, but it wouldn't budge.

Konstantin pointed at Bob, whose eyes were bulging, said, "Stay where you are."

Bob nodded, went to pour more lager down his throat. Realised his glass was empty. Put it on the table. Grabbed George's and finished that too.

"What do you want?" asked Bob, still pale. George was whimpering now.

"Answers," said Konstantin.

"I've as many of those as you want."

"Good. Very sensible decision."

"I heard a scream, what's going on?" said Katrina, back behind the bar.

"Nothing," said Konstantin. "It's a nice time for a walk."

She looked at the screwdriver, left without another word.

"Talk," said Konstantin.

"What do you want to know?" said Bob.

"Who you are, where you live. Stuff like that."

Bob spilled his guts for the next few minutes. Revealed he was foreman of a roadside gang who repaired roads. Occupied caravans adjacent to motorways and A roads. Moved with the job. Ate roadkill to keep costs down. All cash-in-hand work. So they were off the grid. Invisible.

Bob said, "All of us in hiding."

"Getting away from what?"

"Me? Debt. I owe some guys a lot of cash. I'm dead if they find me. So they won't."

"Did George ever tell you why he was there?"

A shrug from Bob. "Speeding tickets." He furrowed his brow. "That's not true, is it?"

"No. He abused and raped his sister for several years."

"For fuck's sake. That's sick."

"You didn't know?"

"No way!" Bob was vehement.

"Because if you did and you agreed to help George, you're as bad as him, in my book."

"Look, I swear, *swear* I knew nothing until you told me."

"If you're lying, I'll find you."

Bob nodded, jowls jangled.

"Get out," said Konstantin. Told him where the van and his boys was hidden. "Don't come here again."

160

Bob went to the door. Undid the bolts, went outside into the bright light. Didn't look back. Was probably already running.

"What are you going to do with me?" said George finally.

"We're going for a ride." Konstantin pulled the screwdriver out of the table. George passed out.

A Pleasant Trip By Boat

The little vessel bobbed alarmingly. It was a motor boat, tiny cabin partially open to the elements. Loud engine set to the rear and hidden under a rough wooden box with an inset hatch. Not much else to speak of.

Other than George, who lay curled up on the deck where Konstantin had thrown him half an hour ago.

"Far enough," he said.

The revs decreased, then died as Fidelity turned the engine off. Sudden silence. Just waves striking the hull. The Russian pulled George to his feet. The man was slumped over, eyes scrunched shut. Like he was agoraphobic and standing on the pinnacle of the Shard.

"Look," ordered Konstantin.

Reluctantly, George did. Immediately threw up over the side. Konstantin let him retch for a minute or two. He was bereft of sympathy. Pulled him to his feet again. Cut the ropes lashing George's wrists together. The wound had stopped bleeding now. At least the water coming over the side was washing it away.

"What are you going to do?" asked George.

"You're going for a little dip," said Konstantin.

"I can't swim. I hate the water!"

"I know."

"But I'll drown!"

"Maybe, maybe not. You're getting more chance than Fidelity had."

"We must be a couple of miles out!"

Which was true. The coastline was visible, but low on the horizon. Konstantin shrugged, said, "So you've something to aim for."

George struggled fiercely as Konstantin dragged him to the rear of the boat. There was a small flap there, cut into the gunwale, which was already open. Konstantin took George right to the deck edge, his feet extended over the water, the waves soaking him to the calf.

"You want to do it?" said Konstantin over his shoulder.

Fidelity knew the plan, had thought it a good one. It wasn't murder. Not really. But she shook her head. Couldn't quite bring herself to do it.

"Wait!" yelled George. "I've a last request!"

"This isn't the movies," said Konstantin.

"My dog. Someone needs to look after Mutt."

"Where is he?"

George told him, then hit the water with a splash after a firm shove in the back. He came up to the surface, gasping. Began to flail his arms in a panicked attempt to stay afloat.

The engine started as Konstantin shut the flap. The boat swung around and headed back to shore. Konstantin tossed the screwdriver. It sank to the depths.

The Russian Has Wheels

"So you've got some wheels at last then?" said Fidelity. The pair was standing at the front of Kathy's house.

Konstantin nodded. Patted the handlebars of the Bullet. "It's a classic."

"No, it's crap."

He shrugged. Didn't care. He liked the name, appreciated its shabbiness and veiled abilities.

"You're staying?" he asked.

A nod from Fidelity. "For now. I left in a hurry before. I don't want to do that again."

"Fair enough."

"What about the dog?"

"I'm taking him with me." Konstantin rested a hand on the German Shepherd's head. The beast barely noticed, tongue lolled out his mouth.

"How?"

Konstantin looked from the dog to the motorbike, said, "I'll figure it out. I'm not leaving either behind."

She stepped closer, reached up on tiptoes and kissed Konstantin on the chin.

"Thank you," she said.

"For what?"

"Everything."

He shrugged, said, "Stay in touch."

"I will, promise."

The last Fidelity saw of Konstantin was him trying to coax the dog onto the Bullet. She laughed to herself. Closed the door.

Infidelity

Hometowns

Through a gap in the curtains, she watched the Russian. He swung a leg over the crappy looking frame of his newly acquired Royal Enfield Bullet, then got the dog on board too. The engine blared into life, throaty growl rattled down the exhaust. Konstantin threw a glance at the house, Fidelity thought she caught a smile. Then he gunned it, released the brake and roared off. She believed she could still hear the reverberation of the souped-up motorbike five minutes later.

Fidelity went outside, walked out towards the sea and stood looking at the waves as they beat at the stone beach, the wind whipping her raven hair about her face. But she didn't really notice them.

Tried to forget Konstantin, but couldn't.

"You're leaving too, aren't you?" said Kathy, Fidelity's aunt. She was bent over the cooker, stirring a pan with a wooden spoon. Kept her back to Fidelity. Smelled like pea soup. Made her feel hungry, as if mere food could fill the pit in her stomach. Out in the hall a clock ticked. Marked the awkward moments.

Fidelity folded her arms across her body, leant back against the door frame. She nodded, "I know I've only just got here, but there's one more thing I need to do before I can move on."

"The other one?" said Kathy. She twisted a knob on the cooker to reduce the heat. Turned around. Fidelity let her arms flop to her side, no resistance left. Gave another nod of her head. Her aunt crossed the floor of the small kitchen, flung her arms wide as she did so. Enveloped Fidelity in a powerful hug. After a heartbeat, Fidelity reciprocated.

"The soup's burning," she said.

"I don't care," said Kathy.

It hadn't taken long to pack. Fidelity simply threw the clothes she'd brought back into the bags, no order to it. Crumpled on top of folded. Dirty mixed with clean. Very unlike her.

Kathy stood waiting at the foot of the stairs, gave Fidelity a broad smile and one last hug when she reached the bottom. No need for words.

Fidelity pulled the weatherbeaten door to behind her. No goodbyes from Kathy either. She gazed around this little piece of Dungeness one last time, knew she'd never return despite what she'd said to her aunt.

She'd miss the solitude, the vast expanse of sea and sky and most of all the sound of the waves on the stones, the wind as it blasted this tiny, hidden corner of the world. But the elements couldn't wash away the fact that this place held too many bad memories for her. One more added yesterday.

Tossed the bags in the boot of the rusty heap of shit Konstantin had borrowed to bring her here. At some point she'd need to return it to the rightful owner. But not right now. Things to do, people to kill. Well, person actually.

The car itself looked fucked, actually it mostly *was* fucked, but it drove fairly well, as long as you kept the speed down. Otherwise a disturbing rattle deep within the structure kicked off. Actually it was a death trap, but beggars can't be choosers as she'd recently been told.

The hinges creaked as she slammed the door closed. There was a wicked draught through the gap where the seal had long ago failed, but Fidelity barely noticed it.

Twisted the key in the ignition, mentally crossed her fingers. The engine burst into life straight away, the one aspect that was well looked after, the hunk of metal within the bonnet fairly gleamed. After all, a car was useless if it couldn't go places.

She performed a three point turn in the narrow road. Went up onto the verge, tufts of hardy grass poking through stone. Traffic here was limited, so there was no rush. Drove through the village. Past the lifeboat station, past the pub. Under the myriad electricity pylons still connected to the defunct nuclear power station.

As she left the boundary of Dungeness the wind gave her one last shove, a blast rocking the car. Fidelity smiled. It was a fitting goodbye.

Fidelity drove for a couple of hours. Stopped once to refuel the car and herself. Had a piss, grabbed a coffee. The shit vehicle got some amused looks from other drivers who'd parked up for a break. She gave them a wave as she pulled out, back onto the motorway. Was *way* beyond giving a fuck what others thought of her.

She felt tired by the time she arrived at her destination. The country's industrial heartland. The lack of mod cons had finally got to her. Jerky suspension, broken seat springs, constant smell of fuel. She cracked a window to let the fumes out. Had to wind it down, such was the age of the car.

Steered the rusty heap of shit into the town centre, immediately felt her hackles rise. She'd have to be careful, the local population would nick anything, even a clunker such as hers.

The place hadn't changed much. Work had dwindled and unemployment risen years ago when the pits had closed. The name Margaret Thatcher still generated bile and hatred up here. Nobody voted Tory.

She noticed there were a lot of charity shops open now. Seemed that every other store had been taken over. British Heart Foundation, Cancer Research, a dogs' home etc. Was there really such a demand for second hand junk? Fidelity wasn't in the mood for benevolence, in fact quite the opposite. She remembered growing up here, done well at school, despite it all. Had a promising future. Where had it gone?

But she knew where. And why. And who.

Billy Vaughn. Little bastard had taken everything from her – and now she was back to collect it.

Welcome To The Jungle

The truth was Fidelity had absolutely no idea whether Billy was still about these parts or not. She hadn't thought about him until recently. Using the money he'd stolen, Billy should be miles away, living the high life on a sunny beach with blue skies and bluer sea.

But there's one thing you should know about Billy. He's a fucking idiot. Probably pissed the fortune up the wall within weeks and was now eking out an existence as a tramp. Fidelity felt the pit in her stomach open up again at the reminder of Konstantin. Squashed it like a bug.

The second thing to know about Billy was the limitation in his horizons. The town he was born in, the kids he ran around with, the football team he supported were the sum total of his world. Fidelity doubted that would have changed. So sure as eggs is eggs he'd be poor and here.

Fidelity parked the car on a side street, took a calculated risk that lunchtime was too early for thieving. The pubs hadn't been open long so, theoretically, none of the drinkers would be needing transportation back to their council houses. The typical process was that, having spent all their cash on beer, none would want or be able to waste it on a taxi, so they perma-loaned someone else's wheels. As a result, the sensible thing to do was not park your transportation in the car park directly behind any place that sold alcohol, unless you really wanted it to be gone the next day.

Talking of pubs, Fidelity headed to what had been, and hopefully still was, Billy's local, The Red Lion. It sat just off the congested High Street. Looked browbeaten like the rest of the town, had probably never seen better days. Peeling paint, cracked windows, not even a sign outside, just the empty metal frame.

She pushed open the door, crossed the threshold. A grey, curtain like pall of smoke hung from the ceiling. Fidelity sucked the fumes down for a moment, had given up the cancer sticks recently, but hadn't yet lost the olfactory kick she got when imbibing a lungful of second hand fag smoke. Made her really fancy a cigarette, just one.

Shook her head. She was here for Billy. Nothing else. Then she'd fuck off back home. Wherever that was now.

The music was loud. Some thrash metal she didn't recognise. Had to wait a few minutes at the bar while a tattooed guy with unnaturally blonde hair served everyone else, even the old bloke who arrived long after her. The barman wore shorts and a T-shirt, despite the weather.

"Sorry love," the barman shrugged when he eventually arrived. "It's the regulars that pay the bills. What do you want?"

Australian accent, Fidelity thought. *How the hell had he ended up here?*

"Information," she said instead.

He laughed. "Don't get many tourists round here." Seemed to be ignorant of the irony in his words. "You looking for somewhere good to eat? 'Cos you'll be fucking lucky. The chippy on the corner is the best place for miles."

The man on the high stool a couple of feet away chuckled to himself. Head down, he stared into his beer, empty packet of peanuts next to it. Avoided Fidelity's eye when she glanced over.

"I'm after a person."

"Ah, that sort of information." He tapped his nose, winked conspiratorially. "Then you'll have to buy a drink."

"What?"

"You don't get something for nothing round here."

She should have remembered, said, "Oh, yeah. Pint of best then."

This time, her neighbour twisted his head to look at Fidelity. Scrawny, sunken cheeks, claws for hands. Nice suit, beige raincoat. Looked sixty, was probably only thirty. He seemed familiar, but before Fidelity's memory could dredge the depths the barman was back with a glass of dark ale.

"That'll be twenty three quid."

"What?"

"Three for the pint, twenty for the 'information'."

She sighed, dug around in her pocket, handed a couple of notes and coins over. Money she could barely afford.

"About this guy I'm looking for..."

"It'll have to wait," he said. "Now's not the time." Stalked off and served another couple of drinkers before she could form a protest.

"For fuck's sake," she said under her breath. Picked up her pint, sat at a small table with a direct view of the bar.

Plenty of cash rang through the till in the thirty minutes Fidelity hung around at the Aussie's pleasure. She spent the period surveying the other residents of The Red Lion. Mostly wasters. Tried to block out the near-constant dirge of heavy metal music. Played the fruit machine for a bit, lost some money, won nothing. Story of her life really.

Eventually she got fed up. Her drink, which hadn't proved too bad, was long gone. Went to the bar, waved the blonde guy over. He shook his head, carried on pulling at the pump, amber fluid swirling into a grimy glass, shared a joke with the customer who'd momentarily be receiving the liquid refreshment.

Fidelity felt a flare of anger burst into life, said, "Fuck this for a game of soldiers."

Stormed the five feet to the flap dividing front from rear of house, and flung it up. Let it slam back down again once she was through. Sounded like a bomb had gone off. That acquired his attention.

"Hey!" the Aussie shouted, spun around, pouring forgotten. Moments later, breathing was forgotten too as Fidelity clamped her hand around his throat. Had him up against the wall, squashing various highly salted snack based refreshments in the process.

"I'm looking for Billy Vaughn. Where can I find him?"

The guy gurgled. She released her grip. He slumped down, arse on the floor, legs splayed out in a V. Rubbed at his throat. A packet of pork scratchings dislodged itself, landed on his head. She squatted down, glared into his pupils, said, "I can make you look even more of a twat if you like. Really mangle your street cred, Bruce. It's up to you."

"It's Greg actually," he said.

"Whatever. I couldn't give a fuck. Spill it."

Greg flicked his eyes off her, looked upwards and past her. Fidelity didn't take the bait. Wasn't going to be distracted.

"Well?"

"Try the town hall," he said eventually.

"Now that wasn't so hard after all."

"Fuck you very much."

Fidelity smiled to herself. Stood upright. Returned to her seat, grabbed her coat. Put her empty pint glass on the bar out of courtesy. Which was more than could be said for the scrawny guy. He'd left three quarters of a pint behind...

Purveyor of Illusions

The town hall was a decrepit building. Had once been painted white, was now only decorated by the feral pigeons that clustered around the multitude of nooks and crannies, shitting on people's heads whenever they had the chance. The public facility just about summed its town up. What should be the premier edifice was instead a dump. Where junkies and prostitutes hung out, almost outnumbered by God squad members of various affiliations, each trying to save the souls of the damned. Fidelity would bet that some of the saviours had become lost themselves.

Fidelity stared at the poster glued on the wall. It was one of many, haphazardly piled one on top of the other, in a stack half an inch thick. His face had been graffiti'd, a moustache and a couple of scars scrawled on. But it was definitely him. A bit more of a tan, whiter teeth, darker perhaps dyed hair. But photos could be manipulated. The glasses, now they were a definite affectation. Unless Billy's eyesight had deteriorated in the past five years. She'd have to see him in real life to know what was real and what was fake.

He'd obviously found a new direction in life too. Now he was a clairvoyant. Seemed to deliver the promise of 'voices from beyond the grave'.

Well, Fidelity thought, *he could find out for himself soon enough.*

Once she got her hands on him.

She checked her watch. The performance wouldn't start for another couple of hours yet. Time to kill. As she was turning away, Fidelity caught movement out of the corner of her eye. Turned to see the scrawny guy pop out of an alley beside the building. He went left, away from her and the hall. Didn't think he'd seen her.

Intrigued, Fidelity entered the passage. It was dim, most of the natural light blocked out. Although there were lamps, all the bulbs had been smashed. The small-time criminals wouldn't want their trade to be observed. She could just about see a couple more of the posters on the wall, further scrawls spray-painted on the grey concrete. Stuff underfoot she didn't even want to even think about identifying.

Only a mercifully short distance to some steps and a railing. A door too, with an illuminated sign that actually worked. Said, 'Stage Door'.

No handle on the outside, could only be opened from within. Otherwise the alley was a dead end. So mister scrawny had to have been in the hall, but seeing who?

Fidelity thought she could hazard a guess. Perhaps her element of surprise was gone.

Ah well. She didn't like revelations anyway. They were for children.

And idiots.

Come Into The Light

She sat at the rear of the auditorium, which was surprisingly packed out. Mostly with old women, very few men. Which just shows the longevity statistics were correct after all. Round here at least.

Fidelity had happily accepted the seat that had 'a restricted view' as the kid at the ticket office had told her. His relief was evident when she'd said yes without an argument. Must have had plenty of complaints in the past.

And once seated she could see why. An ornate pillar stretched from floor to ceiling in front of her. If she'd been bothered about catching the show, Fidelity would have had to crane her neck at dangerous angles to do so. Fortunately, she wasn't interested, wasn't there for the performance.

There was a lot of chatter when she took her seat. But once the lights went down a dead silence descended on the audience. Even the frantic sucking of boiled sweets stopped.

The sound of footsteps on wood reverberated around the space. Then a spotlight flicked on, a cone of white light illuminated a man in a sharp suit, one hand raised, couple of fingers pressed to his bowed forehead.

One glance confirmed it was Jimmy. Bastard seemed to have aged well. Or had undergone plenty of plastic surgery. His teeth really did glint in the powerful glare of the overhead lights. The glasses enlarged his eyes, and his hair, once a greasy mop, was expensively sculpted into a fashionable style that looked like a wave breaking over his forehead.

After a few moments he raised his other hand, which clutched a microphone, whispered, "The spirits are strong tonight. Many people want to be heard."

A ripple ran through the crowd. A tumult of excited whispering.

Seriously? thought Fidelity, looking up and down the row. *They actually believe this bollocks?*

Jimmy was speaking again, a frown of concentration across his forehead. "There's someone coming through. He's a man, strong. His name, it begins with a… D, I think."

The lights flicked up then. No one had taken the bait.

"Worked in the mines," Jimmy tried again. "Known as a bit of a rogue.

Fidelity snorted. That wasn't much of a leap. All the men in this town, when the pit had been open, either dug coal or robbed for a living. Sometimes both. Now it was just the latter. The old biddies, though, they were lapping it up. Nervous laughter in the rows, like they were playing bingo with the spirit world.

"Does anyone recognise this person?" asked Jimmy, staring intently through his glasses, eyebrows creating a deep V as he wrestled with the ghostly plane. "Or it might be a B. Sometimes it's hard to hear the spirits properly."

Beneath her there was some nudging going on. One woman cajoling another. When her friend didn't react, the blue rinse on the left stuck her arm up, wiggled her hand. Was fair bouncing around in her seat.

Jimmy latched onto her, said, "Madam, is this person familiar to you?"

"Yes love, unfortunately."

"Your husband?"

"No, hers." Blue rinse jerked a thumb to her right. Her friend, wearing a hat that would be better suited on a tea pot, looked like she wanted to sink into her seat.

"What was your husband's name?" asked Jimmy.

When the tea cosy woman shook her head, blue rinse stepped into the void. "Bert."

Which meant his given name would have been Albert, confirming to Fidelity what shite this all was.

Jimmy was off again though, reeling his dupe in, said, "And his job?"

Blue rinse laughed, "Too idle for work he was. Got hurt in an accident down the pits and claimed disability the rest of his natural. Lived it up down the pub, he did. Good riddance the day he went, I can tell you."

"Maude!" said Bert's wife, glared daggers and swords at her friend.

"Well it's true! You tell me it's not!"

As the pair began to bicker Jimmy struck the thoughtful, constipated pose again. The lights dropped, the spotlight blinked on. This time clairvoyant Jimmy contacted a woman, the deceased wife of one of the few men in the audience. He burst into tears at the revelation. Started shouting his apologies for all the bad things he'd done in life. Sounded like a long, long list of misdemeanours.

Next up, Jimmy communicated with a bloody dog, of all things.

"For fuck's sake," she mumbled. Got hushed by the woman sitting next to her. Looked like she was shaping up to raise a hand to Fidelity when the lights dropped again. One more farcical dalliance with the otherworld and she'd leave, she decided.

"Ah," said Jimmy. "This is very sad." He rubbed his eyes under his glasses. Looked like brushing tears away. "A little girl. Tiny. Not even born. It's hard to understand her, of course, but the name is coming through. Dawn, I think. Yes, definitely Dawn."

Fidelity's head shot up. He couldn't be doing this. No, surely not. But he was. This time the lights hadn't been raised, the spot stayed firmly on Jimmy, his shoulders hunched over, head bowed so far into the microphone his face was barely visible.

"Poor little mite. Didn't have a chance at life, terminated by her mother before she could emerge into this beautiful world. Does anyone recognise this poor lost soul cast who was cast away from God?"

The spotlight jerked off Jimmy, swung across the audience to settle on Fidelity. The column cut off some of the glare. She was half in, half out of the brilliance. In limbo. Neither above with the angels, nor below with the devil.

Fidelity sprang out of her seat, began fighting her way forward, ready to strangle the bastard. Then everything went fuzzy, but she could still hear Jimmy's voice. Perhaps she'd died, crossed over and that bastard was trying to connect with her.

Which meant there was such a place as hell.

Jimmy Up Close

Fidelity blinked in the light, then jerked backwards. The eyes were huge, massively enlarged by the stupid glasses.

"Take them off, Jimmy. They make you look like a twat," she said, tongue thick in her mouth.

The clairvoyant smirked, but slid the bins off his nose. "I got the idea from a Harry Potter film," he said.

"Sounds like your level," said Fidelity, cringed as a pain shot through her skull. Looked around through slitted eyes. Seemed to be a changing room, probably backstage. Couple of chairs, table pressed up against the wall above which a mirror was fixed, light bulbs around its circumference, several 'congratulations' cards on the table top. Cramped, not a lot of additional space.

"One of my fans took exception to your attempt to minister violence on my soul," said Jimmy. He was even speaking like an idiot now. "Hit you on the pate. A parasol, I think it was."

"Remind me to return the favour next time I see the bitch."

"I doubt there will be a next time."

"Why?"

"Because you're not welcome here," said a different voice. It floated over her shoulder. Ignoring the pain, she twisted around. The scrawny guy from the Red Lion, leaning against the wall in a nonchalant pose. If he'd been wearing a hat and smoking he'd have looked like an extra in a Bogart film. She wasn't surprised he was here, couldn't explain why. Head hurt too much.

"You don't remember me, do you?" he said. Fidelity shrugged, because she didn't care, thinking what to do next. He continued, "There's a balance here. Everyone has a slice of the action, but that's all. Anyone steps on someone else's toes, then that's trouble for them."

"I haven't stepped on anyone's toes," she said.

The scrawny guy smiled, no warmth in it. "But you intend to."

"I'm only here for what I'm owed."

"And I'm only here to tell you to fuck off back to where you came from. We're expecting big things from Jimmy."

Fidelity laughed, even through her pain, said, "The only big thing you can expect from that piece of shit is a screw up of monumental proportions."

Jimmy looked pissed, but didn't say anything. Interestingly, neither did the scrawny guy.

"He owes me," she said.

The scrawny guy sighed. "Look love, take the hint. Go away or you'll get hurt. Okay?"

Fidelity glared at him, hated being called 'love' or any other such derogatory phrase.

"Okay," she lied, "I'll go first thing in the morning. I've had a long drive here. You know what it's like for us women. Short on stamina."

"That's not what I'd heard," said the scrawny guy. Laughed. Jimmy half-heartedly joined in.

She forced down the anger that blossomed in her chest, which threatened to make her lose control. Rip the little bastard's head clean off his shoulders. Shit down his gaping neck.

"People change," she said.

"That's very true. Look at me, used to be the best looking guy at our school."

Fidelity didn't say anything. Scrawny guy sighed.

"Want me to recommend somewhere to stay?" he asked.

"No. Thanks. I'll find my own way."

"Suit yourself." He pushed himself off the wall, walked to the door, half opened it. Looked back over his shoulder, said, "Just be sure to be gone by 8.00am."

"What, no chance of a lie in?"

Scrawny laughed. "Okay, as I'm feeling generous, make it 9.00am then. But no later. We'll know. Come on, I'm not leaving you here with Jimmy."

He crooked his finger. Stepped out the way to let Fidelity pass. She glared down at him. He slammed the door.

Outside in the alley, scrawny guy said, "Wait a moment. You don't know everything."

Fidelity ignored him, carried on walking.

He grabbed hold of Fidelity's arm, brought her up short. She considered snapping his fingers off, stuffing them up his nostrils, but refrained for now.

"I said there's more you should know. It's essential you do."

"Do you mind taking your greasy hand off me? Before I rip you to pieces."

"You always were the most aggressive one at school. Even worse than the lads."

"Do we know each other?"

He shrugged, said, "I know you and that's all that counts. And while we're reminiscing, do you remember the Stanley twins?"

Who didn't?

The scrawny guy filled her in and Fidelity didn't like what she heard.

School Daze

The Stanleys.

Fuck.

Fidelity sat in her shitty car, thinking hard. Deciding whether to leave town and never come back, or stay and face certain trouble.

She'd gone to school with them, a northern version of the Krays. At thirteen years old. Beat up anyone who got in their way, teachers and pupils alike. Sold drugs, sold girls and boys, traded information. You name it, they were into it. The school was theirs. Even the authority figures ran scared of them.

They were about as non-identical as twins could get. As if they had different fathers, created from different sperm. Which was entirely possible, given their mother was rather a prolific prostitute at the time. One kid had stupidly pointed out this possibility. Which happened to be the last time he spoke. Lost his tongue, rather carelessly. The culprits were never caught, although it was rumoured the muscle was kept in a jar of formaldehyde (stolen from the school labs) in one of the twin's bedrooms.

Which led to another peculiarity. No one used or could remember the twins' Christian names. Their mother certainly didn't. Too off her face on a cocktail of class As. Nobody would ask and they didn't tell.

The scrawny guy updated her knowledge of them. Now the twins had their digits in every dirty pie in the immediate area and then some. Back then they'd never been what you'd call 'respecters of boundaries'. These days? Sounded like they had none. Things really had changed since she'd cleared out for the capital. And not for the better it seemed.

So – leave or change the plan? Trouble was she'd never been one to run away. Regardless of the cost.

But she needed an angle...

Payback

She found him sitting on the same bar stool. Although the pub was packed, a no-fly zone seemed to be in force around the scrawny guy. Like he was in his own bubble. Fidelity pulled a seat up next to him. Caught Greg's eye, said, "Usual."

The barman rubbed at his neck. It was bruising up nicely, soon be a fantastic palette of colours. Flicked his eyes to scrawny guy.

"Only been here five minutes and already you're acting like a regular," he said, staring into his pint. "Go ahead barkeep."

Greg did and a glass was shoved at Fidelity, spreading a liquid smear across the wood as the contents spilled. She started to get cash out, but was told, "It's on the house."

"I guess this place belongs to the Stanleys?"

"Not many establishments that don't."

Fidelity downed half the pint. Got a look of admiration from her drinking partner.

"Going to tell me your name?" she asked.

"Only if you let me what you're planning."

"Okay."

He looked surprised, like it had been too easy, said, "I'm Porter."

Fidelity clicked her fingers. "I remember you now." Been scrawny back then too. One of the quiet ones, but a demon with his fists. And had a crush on her.

A second pint went down without any further words passing between them. Bodies jostled at the bar, but the space remained around them and whenever they wanted a drink it appeared with the merest of pauses, regardless of the queue, and no one complained.

Eventually Fidelity said, "Jimmy's going to rob a post office for me. Which, presumably, will be owned by the Stanleys."

"I expect so. Does he know yet?

"No. But he will. And I'm going to be with him."

"Ah, now our problem was sufficiently large enough at the outset, but now? Dramatic proportions." Porter flickered a smile.

"What's so special about the little fucker?" said Fidelity.

"I could ask you the same."

"You first."

"Round here you only take a shit if it's agreed up front with the twins. Jimmy failed to. So he owes them. Fortunately for Jimmy's near-term life expectancy one of the twins is a believer, convinced spirits really do exist and Jimmy's for real. It's their birthday soon and he's the star turn."

"Do you believe?"

"When I'm around the Stanleys I'll have faith in whatever's necessary to stay in one piece and above ground."

"What happens to Jimmy after the anniversary celebrations?"

Porter shrugged, said, "Depends how well he does. Whether he's welcomed back for an encore or not." He had a drink. "Why the robbery?"

"He stole £10,000 from me. I want it back."

"He hasn't got that sort of money."

"Not surprised, he always was too keen on the gee-gees. That's why he's going to steal it for me. And Jimmy, for all his faults, is a good thief."

"Even though I can guess, where do I come into all this?" Porter's smile dipped away.

Fidelity played her only card, said, "Talk to the twins for me."

You're Not In There, Son

Fidelity was woken by a tap at the window. The glass was fogged, so she rubbed at it with a sleeve.

Greg stared in. Cup of something hot in his hand, steam rising off it. Fidelity cranked the window, took the mug.

"You can get a shower if you like," he said.

She'd slept in the shitty car in the overgrown space behind the pub, no cash left for even the crappest of pads. She had a back ache, a crick in her neck and body odour an alley cat would kill for.

"Okay," she said. "But no funny business."

"Thought hadn't crossed my mind."

She grabbed a bag out of the boot, headed inside.

"God, that feels good," said Fidelity to herself as the near scalding water blasted over her skin. It was one of those wide head, power showers. Plenty of knobs to twist, resulting in jets coming at her from all angles.

Once she'd shampooed and soaped her entire body, Fidelity stood for a moment to shake out the knots. The touch on her arse came as a total shock. She spun around, which broke the contact and came face to face with Greg, grinning ear to ear. He was stark bollock naked too.

"What the fuck?" sputtered Fidelity.

"Thought I'd come and join you, work up a lather together," he said. Put his hand out again, this time seemingly going for a breast.

"Fuck off!" she shouted.

Greg's face twisted into fury. "What's wrong with you? It's what you want, I know you do."

Fidelity head-butted the Aussie, planted the crown of her skull into his nose, which splintered under the impact. He wailed, grabbed at his ruined beak, sagged onto the floor. The water turned crimson as blood flowed freely between his fingers. She stepped over the prostrate barman, who now only had his attention set on his pain. Fidelity wrapped a towel around herself, leaned back in, turned the taps to cold, shut the door. Smiled at his wail.

She was drying her hair in one of the bedrooms when Porter turned up. Single bed, magnolia walls, small window with wrinkled curtains blanking out a bleak view of the high street.

"I understand there was some trouble," he said. Fidelity could hear the hum of traffic now the dryer was switched off.

"Wanker shouldn't have tried it on with me, then he wouldn't have got himself hurt."

"I couldn't agree more. He'll be gone by the end of the day, don't you worry. Can't have that sort of behaviour, bad for business."

"I'm not worried. If he touches me again I'll break his fucking arm."

"Yes, I'm sure you would." He scratched at his nose, said, "So I've got you an audience with the Pope. Or more accurately, Popes."

"You couldn't persuade them?"

"The twins want to hear it from you, not the hired help." Porter smiled deprecatingly.

"Let me finish getting dressed."

Porter stayed where he was until Fidelity's glare became too much for him.

Stanley Knives

"So explain to me why we should let you do this," said one of the Stanley twins. He lounged back on a leather sofa, one leg stretched out, the other on the floor. Held a can of beer in hand, something with a foreign name, even though it was early.

If truth be told, he didn't appear dangerous. Most likely due to the ginger hair. But not abetted by bent teeth. Or pasty skin. Like he never went outside.

His brother, in contrast, looked nothing like him. Taller, dark haired, reasonably good looking and knew it. Probably consumed expensive male cosmetics. Drilled in a gym. He nursed a mineral water. Fidelity hadn't been furnished with refreshments of any kind before Porter departed. Her throat was dry from the over-efficient air-con.

The twins occupied the entire top floor of a decrepit block of flats, most of the walls knocked down to make one large residence for the pair. The tall slab of concrete loomed over the town's edge, the last of three originally built in the 1950s. Fidelity could remember when the other two had been demolished, its residents dispersed. Some of her friends were forced to move away. Now all that remained were overgrown hillocks of the rubble remnants.

But this one block endured, thanks to the pair. They'd been born here, grown up in its shadow. A large bribe to a bent councillor on the planning committee and the other necessary votes had been gained via blackmail. Friends, family and the favoured few occupied the other floors.

And now, temporarily, Fidelity. She said, "He owes me money."

"And why do we give a fuck about that?" said the ginger one. "Me and my brother was put on this earth for our profit, not yours."

"You'll get a third of the cut, equal shares."

"But there's two of us, so we want 50%," said Preener.

"That's not fair."

"Okay, we'll make it 75% for us, 25% for you two."

"All right, I'll live with 50%."

"You still haven't convinced us of the why," said Ginger.

"My spirit guide told me I couldn't fail."

Ginger dropped his leg off the sofa, leant forward, hunched over, said, "You what?"

The Preener rolled his eyes. So it was clear to Fidelity which was the believer and which wasn't. She focused on the ginger one. With a hair colour like that she could understand why he'd be sucked in by such bollocks.

"My spirit guide. Said I should pull a job. And I'd get away with it."

"Your spirit guide," repeated Preener, derision clear.

"Don't fucking start," said Ginger, needles in his voice. "If she says that's what happened, it did."

"Ah, for fuck's sake!"

Ginger ignored his brother said, "Carry on, love."

Fidelity gritted her teeth, had to ignore the slight.

"I want to hit a post office."

"In our manor."

Fidelity nodded.

Ginger looked at his brother. Got a half-hearted shrug in response. Preener looked irritated, like he wanted the discussion over. Got up and went to stare out the floor to ceiling window at fuck knows what.

"Well we've a better idea," said Ginger. "Two birds with one stone, like."

"So you're ok with this?" she asked.

"If the spirits are, we are."

There was a loud snort from the twin at the glass. Ginger ignored the scorn.

"What's this other idea then?"

"There's a bookies we know of. Loaded with cash."

"A competitor?"

Ginger nodded his head, said, "Not one of the club. Yet…"

Jimmy Does A Runner... Almost

Fidelity navigated her shitty car through a considerably shittier static caravan park. The thoroughfare was little more than a rutted, muddy track. Faces peered out from behind net curtains fixed across windows. Men, fags in mouth, leaned against door posts following her progress. Kids sat on rusty bikes gave her the finger. Rusty trampolines, rusty cars on blocks. Everything in the park looked brown.

"What a fucking dump," she muttered to herself. "Pleasant lot," she said as another kid saluted with the middle digit.

"It's not you they don't like," said Porter from the passenger seat, "it's me. Or more specifically, my employers."

"They don't like the Stanleys?"

"No one *likes* the Stanleys, they're murdering, thieving bastards."

"Fair comment."

They car bounced through a particularly large pothole, hidden by a puddle of muddy water.

"How much further?" asked Fidelity.

"Leave it here, we'll walk the rest of the way."

She parked up. Fidelity couldn't secure it because the locks didn't work, except the boot. That suffered the opposite problem.

"This way," said Porter.

Fidelity endured a mercifully short walk across swampy ground to reach Jimmy's caravan. It too was shabby, at best. An old sofa sat to the right of the door, stuffing leaking out of many tears in the fabric, as if a dog had been savaging it. To the left was a barbecue, leant over at a perilous angle because of a missing leg.

Porter hammered on the door with the side of his fist. Waited a few seconds and repeated. No answer. Porter raised an eyebrow. Tried the handle. It turned, but with a squeak. Stepped inside. Fidelity followed.

There was a strange odour about the interior. Decay. Unwashed bodies. Damp pets. It was also a mess. Furniture turned over, cupboard doors open, clothes strewn around. Fidelity and Porter searched the caravan, didn't take long. Only a couple of rooms to go through.

Jimmy was gone.

Back outside in the relatively fresh air, one of the kids leant on a BMX that had seen better days two decades ago.

"You're after Jimmy," he said. Wasn't a question.

Porter nodded.

"He paid me not to tell you where he went."

"Okay."

"Are you going to give him a kicking?"

"Probably."

The kid smiled, pointed. "That way."

As Porter and Fidelity ran in the direction he indicated, the kid shouted, "Give the wanker one from me!"

They caught him trying to get over a fence. Fidelity waited, watched him struggle. Six feet up in the air, one trouser leg snared in barbed wire. The only item that had managed to make an escape was his bag, which wallowed in a puddle the far side of the chain link fence.

Eventually Jimmy said, "Bit of help here?"

"No," said Porter.

The Job

Half an hour later, a muddy and bedraggled Jimmy cuddled a mug of steaming tea in a local greasy spoon. Fidelity watched him sip the scalding liquid, grimace, then slop another couple of sugars in.

"That's better," he said.

Jimmy was wedged into a corner, behind a table bolted to the floor, hemmed in by Porter. Fidelity sat opposite. Itched to punch him in the teeth.

"Can I get something to eat?" asked Jimmy. Fidelity noticed the affected prose had been dropped.

"No," said Porter.

"Is that all you ever say?"

"No."

"Why did you run, Jimmy?" asked Fidelity.

"Got a call, told me I was supposed to be doing a job. I don't wanna go back to prison. Someone as pretty as me really suffers inside."

"Who called you?" said Fidelity.

"Dunno. Some Aussie-sounding fucker."

Fidelity glared at Porter.

"Well lucky for you we caught up," said Porter. "Otherwise it'd have been a nasty case of torture, followed by a lingering death." Jimmy went paler, if that were possible. "But don't worry, we'll not tell the Stanleys you tried to screw them over."

Jimmy went a paler shade of bleached.

"Want to hear what the job is?" said Fidelity.

He shook his head, but found out anyway. Afterwards Jimmy said, "Is it too early to get pissed?"

Buckshot

"I don't want to be the driver," said Fidelity.

"You've got the keys," said Porter.

"Because it's my car."

"And I've got the shotgun."

"I'll drive," said Jimmy from the back seat of the shit brown rust bucket.

Fidelity and Porter responded in tandem, said, "Shut up!"

"I only offered," grumbled Jimmy, twisted away to direct his sulk out the dusty window.

"This wasn't the plan," said Fidelity.

"Well the plan's changed. You're the driver, that's final," said Porter. "Let's get going. We've got a drive ahead of us."

Fidelity twisted the key in the ignition. Started first time.

She parked right outside the bookies, a real slice of fortune as the narrow street was rammed out with abandoned vehicles. Kept the engine running. Even though it always started without fail, there was always a first time. It couldn't be now.

"Masks on," said Porter.

The trio pulled balaclavas down hiding their features. The cheap material irritated Fidelity's skin. She immediately started to heat up, perspiration prickled her neck and back.

"Let's go," Porter told Jimmy.

"Do we have to?"

"We'll be in and out before you know it."

"Oh fucking hell!" Jimmy took a deep breath, yanked at the door handle, then was out on the street. Porter joined him a moment later.

Fidelity glanced in her rear view mirror. The road relatively deserted, a couple of smokers outside the pub, backs turned to her. They shivered in the cold weather, would be inside as soon as they could. Otherwise the buildings consisted of terraced houses squashed together and a tiny store.

When Fidelity dropped her eyes from the mirror, Porter and Jimmy were gone. She rattled her fingertips on the pitted steering wheel, looked at her watch, glanced up to the rear view. The smokers must have re-entered the pub.

Then she heard two blasts in quick succession, the heavy boom of a shotgun. Then the lighter sound of a handgun, several bullets being fired. Then the shotgun again.

Deathly silence until the screaming started. Fidelity kicked her door open, left it yawning, engine still turning over. She burst into the bookies. Lifted the balaclava up to forehead level. Couldn't believe her eyes. The interior was utter carnage. Jimmy lay flat on his back to her left. Half his face gone. He'd crossed over. Blood was already pooling around him.

Directly in front, a basic counter stretched across most of the shop's width. A couple of televisions mounted high up on the wall, one showing football, the other smashed.

Over the buckshot-peppered bench stretched a body, face down. Arms dangled towards the floor where a pistol lay, still smoking. She went over, touched fingers to his neck. No pulse. Behind the bench was another form, a guy slumped in the corner, blood all over his shirt. She didn't have the time to check him.

Porter had his back to the wall. He was breathing fast, shallow, a hand pressed across his stomach, the other still clutching his weapon. She tugged it out of his grasp. He was too weak to resist. Then pulled off his balaclava. His face was deathly pale, beads of sweat peppered his skin.

"What the fuck happened?" she asked.

"What I expected." Porter grimaced as a wave of pain hit him.

"You knew this was going to happen?"

Porter nodded, said, "Couldn't let you walk into a trap."

"The fucking Stanleys."

"Just one of them."

"Why?"

"Because he wants to prove to his brother that the spirit world isn't real, to break his conviction. So the two people who are supposed to have 'powers' wind up dead, proving it's all bullshit."

"But it is."

192

Porter coughed, said, "You know that, I know that, but the Stanleys are lunatics."

"I'll kill them."

Porter put out a hand, squeezed Fidelity's forearm. "You'll never get near them. Save it for another time. Now get out of here before the cops arrive."

Fidelity shook her head, but knew Porter was correct. She hoisted the shotgun, stuffed Porter's balaclava in her pocket. Put the weapon in Jimmy's hand. Scattered some betting slips around Porter. Maybe the cops would be incompetent enough to think Porter was just a bystander. A slim chance, but better than nothing.

"Go!" he said.

Fidelity squatted down again, kissed Porter on the cheek.

"At least now I can die a happy man," he said.

"You're not going to die."

"Time will tell, now fuck off!"

Fidelity pulled her balaclava back down over her face, hit the street. A small crowd were outside the pub. One pointed at her, was on a mobile phone. Fidelity pulled her car door shut, threw the shotgun on the floor, rammed the car into gear.

Ten minutes later, she tossed the shotgun into a bunch of trees in a lay-by. For now she kept the balaclavas, too much forensic evidence attached. She'd burn them later. She had no reason to go back to town, her bags were in the boot. Trouble was she had no idea where to aim for. She wasn't ready to go to Margate and find Konstantin, too much in her head cluttering it up. Too much in his as well.

Fidelity shook her head, put the car in gear and drove slowly away.

Close
Contact

Prologue
Writes and Wrongs

In a strange way Konstantin missed Fidelity Brown. Like an aching tooth finally extracted, that sense of pleasure from relief, but tempered by recollected pain. It was an odd sensation the Russian had never experienced before.

He'd been thinking for a while that perhaps he should commit some of his past misdeeds to paper. Write some wrongs. And that day seemed to be here. Nothing better to do at the moment. There'd be no chronological order to them, they'd be written simply as and when they came into his head.

Korea, that's where he'd start.

July 1990.

Arrivals

Gimpo International Airport, Seoul, South Korea

Konstantin Boryakov jerked awake as black rubber wheels roughly kissed grey concrete runway, like two drunks in a fumbling embrace. A recent scar on his chest niggled with the jolt, knitted together, but not yet properly healed. A knife wound from a now dead opponent, the man's body disposed of in an incinerator. Every mission left its mark in some way, be it mental or physical.

The plane slewed a little as friction re-exerted its hold, jerked the cabin from side to side. The roar of jets kicked in as the pilot, Konstantin mused he was probably ex-military from the cavalier attitude, reversed thrust to slow the aircraft's headlong rush. Somewhere forward of the Russian came a scream. Either a nervy passenger outwardly displaying their fear, or a hasty expulsion of excitement.

Within seconds the airliner's pace was sufficiently measured so the pilot dropped the engines to a more normal throaty growl, steered the aeroplane off the runway and towards an empty stand. A stewardess made an announcement in Korean, then English. Neither were Konstantin's first language, but nevertheless he was fluent in both.

"Korean Air welcomes you to Gimpo International Airport. Would all passengers remain seated until the plane comes to a complete stop."

Probably a businessman up in first class was already on his feet, keen to get off as quickly as possible, shorten the wait at passport control. Personally the Russian wasn't bothered. He had hours to kill. Whether he did so in a queue or in the *yogwan* he'd booked for his short stay in the country, it didn't matter to him.

The moment the plane drew to a halt, passengers leapt up, drowning out the stewardess as she repeated the welcome to her country, then thanked the passengers for flying with her employer.

Konstantin didn't fight gravity or the rush to exit and remained installed in his seat. Let the chaos swim around him. Only when the corridor was nearly empty did he stand, extract his bags from the overhead locker and make his way forward. A stewardess at the head of the cabin smiled at him.

"Goodbye," she said.

"*Kamsahamnida*," replied Konstantin, to which he received a small smile from the tired looking woman.

He sauntered along the air bridge and into the terminal, feeling the quick burst of heat within the umbilical before the air conditioning wrested back environmental control.

The temperature didn't bother Konstantin. He'd been in the Asia Pacific region for months now on two operations, latterly Thailand. But his trip to South Korea was entirely personal and purely for recreational purposes.

A week of learning a new method of kicking the crap out of other people. Konstantin couldn't think of a better way to spend his downtime.

Out On A Lamb

Mr. Lamb had spent a lot of his working life awaiting a response from Malcolm Dennis. Today was no exception.

To the average passer-by it would have seemed like Mr. Lamb's Head of Section was simply seated on the bench, staring at clouds. A pair of civil servants burning their lunch hour in the mid-summer sun. One shifting towards being overweight, but not ready to admit it by the tightness of his collar and waist, not yet ready to buy a new wardrobe. The other wiry, intense, cold.

But the passer-by would have been utterly incorrect.

Mr. Lamb knew Dennis was contemplating, calculating, assessing input versus output and, critically, risk versus reward. All aligned to a continuation of his steep upward trajectory within the SIS, otherwise known as MI6. The British secret service, so clandestine the public had little knowledge of its workings beyond a raft of fictional spy novels written by ex-agents, the contents of which often sailed a little too close to the truth for comfort.

He observed a mother walk past, pushing a buggy. Within sat a squalling toddler the woman was attempting to ignore. But Mr. Lamb could see from the stony expression on her face she was all too aware of its presence. All he wanted to do was stride over to the infant, comfort it, tell her that life was fragile…

"No."

His boss's verbal missive jerked Mr. Lamb away from past loss, back to the here and now. It took him a moment to register the response was not the one he desired, but had anticipated. He turned a pair of black eyes onto Dennis, regarded him. His Head of Section appeared unfazed, returned Mr. Lamb's gaze with a few percentage points of interest added.

"Why?"

"It serves absolutely no purpose."

"To whom?"

Dennis ignored the rebuke, gathered up a paper bag from the bench, stood and walked the short distance to the lake. Mr. Lamb could hear the rustle as his boss searched within for bread crusts. His arm jerked, a small white lump flew towards the water, followed by a cascade of quacking feathered friends.

Mr. Lamb surmised that this was exactly the behaviour his Head of Section appreciated. Underlings fighting over scraps that he doled out as and when he wished. Ordinarily Mr. Lamb rose well above the internal squabbles, but this time he couldn't. And Dennis knew it. All of this was simply an act, an opportunity for Dennis to turn the screw deeper into Mr. Lamb's heart.

For a moment the agent considered taking Dennis by the throat. Perhaps squeezing the life out of him between his five fingers. Or snapping his neck with a single, quick jerk. Or even a more laboured, inhumane submersion in the lake until liquid, rather than air, filled the man's lungs. Mr. Lamb knew he could do it.

Instead he acquired the spot to Dennis's left, said, "I'll owe you."

Dennis remained impassive, after a couple of moments replied, "And you'll be on your own." It wasn't a question.

"Of course."

His boss said nothing more. Simply manoeuvred the bag in front of Mr. Lamb who, after a moment's hesitation, put his hand within, drew out a crust and tossed it up into the air. The deal was sealed.

And Mr. Lamb knew that if all went wrong, it was down to him. And him alone. Which was just the way he liked it.

There was a debt to settle.

Welcome To South Korea

Today
Passport Control, Gimpo International Airport, Seoul

With the advent of the Seoul Olympics a couple of years ago, what had been a trickle of the more hardy of tourists became a flood. What had been an enigmatic location became familiar once splashed all over the television for weeks on end. The country itself hadn't changed. Simply being on a screen made it seem accessible, normalised the distinct.

So Gimpo was a throng of people on Konstantin's arrival. He stood calmly in the immigration queue, didn't use his diplomatic pass that would have meant a circumvention of the arrivals hall, passport control, baggage collection. Because he was on holiday. The documentation stayed buried deep within his luggage. In a space even the most diligent of officials wouldn't find.

He regarded his fellow passengers. The South Koreans divided from the foreigners in a separate, faster moving line. Saw nothing to interest him. Families, workers, officials. Typical.

It took seventy five minutes of rhythmic and infrequent shuffling to reach the yellow line which could not be crossed until permitted. A uniformed guard six feet away in a glass booth. Beyond, armed soldiers against the wall, their eyes focused on a point in the middle distance.

Then it was his turn. Konstantin shouldered his bag, took three confident steps forward. Handed his papers over. The border guard, a young man with a zealously efficient gaze, read over the customs form first, neatly filled in by Konstantin. Didn't bat an eyelid at the address where the Russian would be staying.

Next flicked through every page in the Swedish, and therefore fake, passport. Took in the stamps, dates of entry and exit. But there was nothing in there that would raise a flag, Konstantin knew. His expression and metabolism remained firmly in neutral.

Eventually the guard reached for a large stamp. Punched it down onto what had been a blank page. Signed a scrawl over the top of the entry and exit dates.

"Welcome to South Korea," he said and handed over the passport without an accompanying smile.

Konstantin nodded his thanks and moved on.

He had a choice between the local rail service or a taxi into the city. He chose the latter, more for simplicity than any other factor. He'd just tell the driver where to go and be taken there. He was feeling a little tired and couldn't be bothered negotiating an unfamiliar transport network. He was on leave, after all.

He headed outside, no checked luggage to collect from the carousel, hunted for a cab. Found the obligatory line of cars, drivers standing around smoking, instead of baking inside the metal shell. As he did so something tapped at his mind, but he carried on going through the motions. Allowed his peripheral vision to soak up the data for later processing.

As Konstantin neared the rank, the driver of the car at the front pushed off his bonnet. Waved at Konstantin, opened the rear door, then went to the boot and popped it, held out his hand. Konstantin shook his head, told the driver he'd be keeping his possessions with him.

The driver shrugged to say it was of no consequence to him. Konstantin threw his bag into the taxi then joined it. The driver slammed the door, climbed in himself, started the engine, then flicked the air conditioning, such as it was, to full blast.

The border guard held his hand up to stop the progress of the next person in the queue. Noted the look of irritation at being forced to wait a moment longer flash across the bespectacled male's face. The guard decided there and then the man would be 'randomly' selected for a full body search. But first he picked up the phone, uttered a few words, cut the call.

With a miniscule grin he crooked a finger. The tourist stepped forward, no clue what he was heading towards.

Forced Entry

Two Days Ago
MI6, London

Back in his office, Dennis checked the quality of the sound recording. Some of the discussion was overlaid with the rustling of his clothing, the sound of some stupid birds in the background, a crying baby. Not perfect, but sufficient for his purposes.

The Head of Section was an accumulator. He hoarded evidence. For and against others. Always to his own benefit. He'd been after Lamb for some time, but the man was too careful, too fucking honest actually.

Until tragedy had struck. Thrown Lamb's moral compass off track. Whether it was permanent Dennis neither knew nor cared, provided his abnormal behaviour lasted long enough for his purposes.

He sent a message to his employee's pager. One word. 'Go.'

Then picked up the scrambler phone and called his opposite number in Moscow.

"Yuri, I hope you are well?"

"Ah, Mr. Dennis. A pleasure, as always," replied Yuri in his excellent, almost accentless English.

Dennis knew this to be a lie, but then Yuri had been superbly trained. They'd attended the same public schools, after all.

"Just to say that the process to handle our mutual issue is under way at my end."

"Excellent!" laughed Yuri. The man's effusiveness made Dennis's skin crawl, always had. Couldn't the man keep his emotions in check?

"I trust you will keep your end of the bargain?"

"Of course. Why would I not? Don't you have confidence in me?"

Dennis forced a laugh, said, "Always, Yuri."

"Good. Then if you will allow me to go, I will attend to my actions."

With an 'au revoir', Yuri cut the call. Dennis softly replaced the receiver, sat back in his chair and hoped it was all going to work out for the best.

Because he'd be fucked if it didn't.

Enter Master Shin

Today
Arrivals, Gimpo International Airport, South Korea

"There he is," said Duncan Hill and stroked his moustache as he did at times like these. He was sitting inside a car parked far enough back from the blocky terminal building to be unobtrusive, close enough to freely observe. The windows were down, allowing some of the heat to exit. He watched the well-built man search for a taxi, a single bag slung over his shoulder.

In the passenger seat, Shin nodded.

"A big guy," said Hill.

Shin shrugged. Hill was used to his counterpart saying very little, but then again he could speak enough for two people.

"Are you clear on the plan?"

"Sure," said Shin.

"Just remember to keep out of sight."

"Of course."

"Okay then, see you later."

Shin got out of the car, shut the door quietly. Hill watched him climb into a battered Hyundai parked a couple of spaces in front. A plume of grey smoke spurted from the exhaust when he started the engine. The Hyundai pulled out and dropped in behind the taxi as it left.

Hill re-entered the terminal building. Found a nondescript door with a brass plaque next to it, four meaningless numbers engraved into the surface. It looked official that way. A key got him inside. A desk, phone, fax machine and a chair which Hill dropped his rotund self into.

He put a call through, waited for it to connect. "He's here."

"I'll be with you soon," replied Mr. Lamb. "Stick to the plan."

"Okay," said Hill, but the wraith-like Lamb was already gone.

Hill shook his head. His friend had changed significantly in the past few months. Where once there had been a sense of humour and warmth for his fellow man behind the professional façade, now there was ice and hate. Hopefully, once this Russian was dead, his friend could find some peace.

But somehow Hill doubted it.

Shin had enjoyed his meeting with Hill. Particularly the fact that he'd had no idea what was going on around him, oblivious to the contents of the boot. If he'd have known he was transporting a corpse, Hill would have wet himself. One of those in-field agents who didn't really undertake any of the dirty work. He was just a messenger really.

But for once Hill had a greater purpose to fulfil. He just didn't know it yet.

Testing Time

Today
Han River Crossing, Seoul, South Korea

The driver looked at Konstantin in the rear-view mirror. A pair of brown eyes in a sallow face. Konstantin told him the destination. The man simply nodded and pulled away, without indicating, and at speed.

Gimpo airport's major benefit was its relatively close location to Seoul, only nine miles to the west of the centre. There was talk of building a new facility to deal with the tourist boom, but on land much further out. Although the ground had yet to be broken.

The taxi soon crossed the Han river via a wide, arrow-straight bridge that cut across sluggish waters. The city hunkered down on the other side, ready to welcome Konstantin. The Russian looked over his shoulder through the back window, then faced forward again and leant back in his seat. Ran over his recollection from outside the airport.

By the time he realised what had caught his attention, or more specifically, who, the driver was pulling up outside the *yogwan,* an inn best described as 'functionally basic'. Konstantin paid the fare, added a tip which the driver barely acknowledged.

Konstantin checked in. Handed over his passport for the second time. He was given a key. The Russian climbed two sets of stairs, found the door to his room and threaded the key into the lock.

The door yawned open to reveal a small space. Its contents consisted of a cushioned mat and a pillow that lay on the floor, or *ondol*, which was warm to the touch. Along with a diminutive cupboard and some shelves. The shared bathroom was a couple of doors down the narrow hallway.

First Konstantin took a look around, wanted to know where the exits were. The floor of the *yogwan* was arranged in a rectangle, the rooms directly off it. At the centre of one side was a set of stairs that led to reception and the street. The stairs also led upwards to another floor and the roof.

The Russian kicked his door closed, dumped his bag on the floor. It was too early to go to the martial arts hall and he had a more pressing aim in mind. He looked out the window, down onto the street. He suspected his taxi had been followed but it was hard to be sure. All the vehicles looked the same.

Konstantin stripped off the trousers and shirt he'd been wearing for the past sixteen hours, threw them in the corner. Pulled on T-shirt, shorts and a pair of battered trainers. Then back outside into the rising heat. He pulled a few stretches, took the time to discern his surroundings while he gently strained his muscles. Headed left for no good reason and began to pound the streets.

He tracked through a residential district, down busy streets awash with market stalls, the aroma of cooking food a heady concoction. Across a business district, more conservative, workers in white, short sleeved shirts, collars buttoned, men seemingly constricted with dark ties. July was proving to be an exceptionally warm month, the temperature barely dropping away at night and today was going to prove no different. Perspiration cascaded. It felt like every pore was in freeflow.

He glanced back, saw the car again. A dent in the bonnet. For most of his run it had stayed well back, but now hugged his heel, the wheels in the gutter while the Russian's feet pounded the pavement. It held him, forced a straight line. Then suddenly the car sprang forward, cut right across his path and jerked to a halt half in, half out of an alley. Two men peeled out of the vehicle, two more from the passage's mouth.

Konstantin drew to a halt. Twisted and saw another couple of guys step out of a shop doorway. All looked capable, broad shouldered, several with previously smashed noses that had been badly reset, every one with a glint in their eyes. Enjoyed a fight. Then again, so did he.

Six to one, not bad odds, thought Konstantin. He'd faced worse.

The Russian took a closer look at his opponents, evaluated them by their stance. Three were clearly Taekwondo practitioners; standing at a 45 degree angle to him with legs shoulder width apart, up on their toes, almost bouncing in readiness. The trio held their arms at two heights, one down to protect the ribs, the other high to protect the head in near copies of each other. It looked impressive, but Konstantin knew taekwondo was about scoring points and knockouts, not causing significant harm or killing your opponent. Gave him a big edge.

Numbers four and five looked somewhat more dangerous, probably trained in Hapkido. Their posture was more closed, arms tucked to bring their elbows in to protect ribs, fists in a striking position.

The final guy, six, hung back, simply waiting. Konstantin figured he'd probably let the others wear him out before attacking. His abilities were an unknown.

Konstantin rolled his neck, then his shoulders. Forgot the pain in his thighs, the constriction across his chest from the recent knife wound. Drew in a couple of lungfuls of air, stuffed oxygen into his already adrenaline fuelled body, kicked it up another notch. In one way it was intelligent to stop him mid-run, in another it was incredibly stupid. He was primed and ready.

In a sudden move the Taekwondo guy nearest Konstantin moved in, threw a roundhouse. The Russian had a split-second to deal with the kick, stepped in and dropped his left arm to protect his body, his right arm up and across to protect his head. He barely felt the blow which rattled uselessly against his limb.

Konstantin grabbed the guy's leg, jerked it up and trapped it between his left shoulder and head. He smashed an uppercut into the sensitive nerves of the perineum region. Lifted his attacker off his feet – Konstantin added to the gravitational pull, slammed him into the ground, head first. There was an audible crack as skull met pavement.

Konstantin felt a hand land on his shoulder, spun him around. The Russian took a fist in the face. The man grabbed Konstantin's collar tugged in an attempt to take him to ground. Konstantin saw a flash in his peripheral vision, the third and final Taekwondo combatant was approaching fast from his right and shaping up for a strike.

Konstantin brought his arms up inside the grasp of the guy holding him. With his left hand he cupped the chin and his right hand went behind his head to grab an ear and a handful of hair. With his weight as a lever, Konstantin swung his opponent into the path of the guy rushing at him who was already committed to a high axe kick. A foot thudded into on the bridge of number two's nose and right eye, knocked him unconscious. Konstantin let him flop to the floor.

Without the slightest concern for his associate, number three threw a high back spinning kick at Konstantin's head. The Russian ducked the movement, stepped within punching range, crushed the man's windpipe with the heel of his hand. Number three began to choke, unable to draw the slightest breath. Pressed his hands to his throat as if that would help. He'd be dead very soon.

Three down, fifty per cent progress, thought Konstantin.

Number four took a more cautious approach. He was the tallest of the lot, a good few inches beyond even Konstantin, which gave him a longer reach and able to stay out of grasp. Konstantin eyed him warily. Checked on the other two, they seemed content to stay back for now. Rotated around the action. Number four threw out a low cut kick. No power in it, simply a test.

Konstantin kept his counsel, shuffled back half a step. His opponent, blood up, took the bait and stepped forward. Konstantin did the same, now within the other man's range, negating his reach advantage. The Russian struck with a crushing back kick to his right rib cage. He felt his foot penetrate, knew he'd broken some ribs. The guy doubled over, grabbed the damaged area and moaned. Konstantin took him out with a rapid knife hand to the base of the skull, where spine and skull join.

Before Konstantin could react he felt an arm wrap around him, constrict his throat. Then a couple of sharp punches into his kidneys. The blows he could live with all day, plenty of muscle in the region, but the hand around his neck was a problem Konstantin tightened his neck, lowered his chin to diminish the grip's progress.

Konstantin reached up with both hands and grabbed the throttling hand, twisted it away out and down. He spun, brought his left elbow up into the side of his opponent's head, putting all of his considerable weight into the blow. Konstantin, now free, stepped in close and crashed a right uppercut into the staggering man. He went down, out cold.

The Russian turned. Looked at the final man. Couldn't resist crooking a finger. *Come on.*

Elicited a smile from his remaining opposition who began to close the gap, stance like a MMA fighter, stocky, powerful. Konstantin mimicked him.

Number six threw a low distance-measuring right leg roundhouse, continued to spin into a jumping turn kick. Konstantin shuttled backwards, just enough to allow the kick to pass in front of his face.

The man landed, but continued spinning, delivered a back fist to Konstantin's head, caught him by surprise. The Russian went down, on his back, stared briefly at the sky. Konstantin rolled backward, lifted up his legs to block an axe kick aimed at his head. Their legs tangled, tripped number six and he flew over the top of Konstantin and onto the ground.

The Russian got to his feet, glad to be off the concrete where he was disadvantaged. His opponent was up too but didn't pause, threw a right punch which Konstantin stepped inside, blocked it with both arms, sliced his right forearm down onto his opponent's collarbone. There was the dull snap of the bone breaking, the man screamed. Konstantin ignored his pain, grabbed an arm, pulled him in close and hip tossed the MMA man upside down and to the floor. Konstantin wrapped a forearm round his neck – choke hold – squeezed the jugular while the other man struggled in his grip. Half a minute and he lapsed into unconsciousness. Fifteen seconds further would produce permanent brain damage, sixty seconds would mean death.

Konstantin let go. Done what he needed to do.

He felt eyes on him. Looked around and caught sight of the original car from the airport. A window was wound down all the way, a face staring back at him, slight smile on his lips. Konstantin registered all of his features, got to his feet, then began running again.

There was a man leaning against his door when Konstantin reached his room. Not a local. He paused in the hallway, hadn't seen anyone else on the stairs. No one outside with the slightest air of suspicion about them. More than likely this one was alone. A messenger then. Not a killer.

"You look hot," he said. In Russian. Which Konstantin hadn't expected.

"Not particularly."

The man jerked a thumb over his shoulder, said, "May we go inside?"

"No."

The other grinned. "I was told you'd be like this."

Konstantin didn't respond. Knew the guy was playing with him.

"Sergey wants to see you."

The Yonggeumok

Today
Yonggeumok Restaurant, Mugyo-dong, Central Seoul

Konstantin nursed a *soju*. He'd asked the waiter to cut the slightly sweet, rice distilled liquor with some green tea. Lied to himself that the tannins would counteract the slew of alcohol. He sat at a low table, its surface only inches above the floor, his backside perched on a bench, legs crossed. Very traditional, surprisingly comfortable.

Sergey Guryanov was late. A good fifteen minutes after the appointed time, the head of South Korea's Russian office entered with two men at his back. He glanced around, immediately saw Konstantin and threaded his way through the diners.

Konstantin had never met the man before, only knew of him by reputation. Of average height, Sergey sported a thin moustache and gold rimmed glasses on a round face. He was broad and walked with the appearance of a strong man.

When Sergey reached Konstantin, a broad grin splashed across his face. "May I?"

"Of course," responded Konstantin.

Sergey nodded to his men, who took up a table nearby. As he settled himself a waiter arrived, said, "Would you like something to drink?"

"The same as he's having," Sergey replied in Korean.

"And some water?"

"Why not? With gas, I think."

Konstantin noted that Sergey hadn't bothered to check first with him. The waiter bowed, retreated.

"Have you looked at the menu?" said Sergey. "The Yonggeumok is famous for its *chueotang*." said Sergey with what sounded like pride in his voice. "It's one of the oldest establishments in the city and opened in 1933. Seoul, it's always changing, always something being knocked down, then rebuilt. People coming, going, dying, being born. But the Yonggeumok holds firm, it's a rock around which everyone else swirls and shifts. You see there's no true centre to Seoul, unlike other capitals. Each district is like a city itself, each with its own centre, which is makes the Yonggeumok so special, such a draw."

The waiter returned then with a tray, placed it on the table, interrupted Sergey's eulogising. He transferred a glass of the *soju* in front of Sergey then took the bottle of water, twisted off the cap which generated a hiss of escaping carbon dioxide. He poured the liquid into two glasses filled with ice. Put them at their right elbows, then the bottle in the centre, cap replaced.

Sergey waved ordered two of the loach soup dishes from the waiter in quick-fire Korean.

"You'll think more clearly after a portion of *chueotang*, let me tell you. Now, where was I?"

"Giving me a history lesson."

Sergey laughed, said, "I'm sorry my friend. I have a passion for the past. It's all too easily forgotten by the young today."

Before Konstantin was able to reply, the waiter delivered two bowls which steamed prodigiously. Thick and brown, the gloop smelt strongly of spices. Konstantin dipped a spoon into the liquid, disturbed a vegetable that appeared to be an onion sliced onto the surface as a garnish. Konstantin lifted the spoon to his lips and sipped cautiously, surprised he enjoyed the vibrant flavours experienced by his tongue.

"How is it?" asked Sergey.

Konstantin nodded. "Good."

"It's supposed to be very healthy," said Sergey, "clears the nose better than a hosepipe. They've pots of the stuff permanently on the go here because it's so popular."

It did seem that pretty much everyone in the restaurant had the same dish. No more conversation passed between the pair until all was consumed.

"Well? Do you feel it?" Sergey breathed in theatrically. "Evacuated lungs!"

"Yes," lied Konstantin

Sergey grinned, clearly delighted his guest had experienced the desired effect. Then he turned serious, dropped the smile, leant over the table as far as he could. He spoke in a low tone, "Now, my friend, let us find out what is troubling you."

Konstantin opened his mouth to speak, but Sergey halted him before he could utter a syllable.

"Do not look so irritated, Konstantin. First I need to know why you're here."

"A holiday to train in Tuk Kong Musul."

"Ah." Sergey sat back, a frown on his face. "Go on."

"It's a martial art."

"I know what it is. Anyone who understands the tensions between North and South Korea does."

Which was true, thought Konstantin.

In the 1960s and 1970s, the North Korean special forces seemed able to mount constant deadly incursions over the border at will. In response, the embarrassed South Korean Special Forces developed the ultimate martial art, blending the best of the existing forms – judo, karate, Taekwondo and Hapkido among others – with one key objective. To take down your opponent as fast and as hard as possible. The result was Tuk Kong Musul.

"A holiday, you say?" asked Sergey.

Konstantin nodded.

"A hell of a way to take a few days off!" Sergey laughed at his own joke. Konstantin forced a smile.

"I'm not exactly the tourist type," said Konstantin.

"No, that is clear." Sergey dropped the grin, leant over the table, lowered his voice. "And this is the only reason you're here? No old scores to settle?"

A frown scoured Konstantin's brow, said, "Should I be?"

"I'm just asking. Well it wouldn't be the first time."

Konstantin shrugged, unwilling to comment.

"Well, I hope you enjoy yourself my friend, and if there's anything I can do to help, just let me know."

"Now you mention it," said Konstantin. "There is something."

Sergey raised an eyebrow.

Shin Lies

Today
Gimpo International Airport, Seoul, South Korea

Mr. Lamb followed in Konstantin's footsteps through passport control. Ordinarily, he too would have used his diplomatic pass to avoid customs – been first off the plane, guided along the air bridge and straight to a nondescript door cut into the corridor which led the sheep to the airport. The door would have shut behind him, killing the hubbub of exiting passengers. Then to a car and a quick exit.

But not today. Because he wasn't supposed to be here.

Mr. Lamb had travelled under a false name. The passport itself was legitimate, as was Jake Francis, but he was long dead, simply a name on a gravestone.

The process took a shockingly long time, during which Mr. Lamb was unable to shut down and undergo the usual low level self-hypnosis to cut out all the chaos around him. Fine on the flight, far too risky here. Too exposed and no safety net. His eyes constantly roved.

Outside he made for the car park in the gathering gloom. Collected a nondescript saloon, left where Hill had said it would be. He found the padded envelope underneath the passenger seat. Inside was a single sheet of paper. And a gun. Mr. Lamb clicked on a small torch, read the address and memorised it. He returned the envelope and its contents back under the seat, doused the light, fired up the engine.

Mr. Lamb manoeuvred the car onto the unfamiliar road that only hours before Konstantin had negotiated.

The man watched the foreigner with the chilling black eyes drive off. Followed at a discreet distance, even though he knew exactly where Mr. Lamb was destined for. His only job was to ensure the foreigner made it, or to report in if he didn't. He fervently hoped the former would be the case, because Master Shin was a far worse prospect.

"This is where he's staying," said Shin, nodded towards the *yogwan*.

"Okay. Any activity with the Russian?" asked Hill.

"No," lied Shin.

"Good, that's what I like to hear."

"What now?"

"We wait for my friend to arrive."

"He's on his way?"

Hill nodded.

"Show me his room."

"Why? There's nothing in it. I've already checked."

Shin smiled and Hill noticed the expression was confined to his lips. The brown eyes remained deep pools.

"Humour me," said Shin.

Hill felt a shiver of anxiety but couldn't put the feeling into cogent thought. But he quashed his doubts, remembered what Dennis had told him – that Shin should be given whatever he wanted.

"Okay," he said and led Shin inside.

Shin Revealed

Yonggeumok Restaurant, Mugyo-dong, Central Seoul

"Yes, I know him," said Sergey, once Konstantin had described the local who'd watched the fight between the Russian and his six men. Konstantin noted any shred of good humour had fallen away from Sergey's features.

"And?"

Sergey sighed, deep and heavy as a dumbbell. "It's not a good situation." He waved at the waiter. Ordered something significantly stronger than the *soju*. He didn't speak again, lapsed into thought.

The waiter returned with a couple of shot glasses and a bottle of a colourless liquid. Placed them on the table and began to pour. Sergey grabbed the bottle from the man's hands, rattled in Korean that the waiter was to leave everything to him.

Sergey poured, drank and poured again.

"What is the matter?" asked Konstantin.

"He is a killer."

"So? We are killers too."

"But this man, he is the worst of them. Wanted all over Asia. If Shin is here, it's for something significant. He commands a huge fee and only takes the biggest of jobs. And he doesn't care who he murders or how. Only two things are important. The money and the conclusion."

"Conclusion?"

"Da. It is critical to Shin that his victims end up dead. He's never failed to complete a contract yet."

"Why would he be interested in me?"

"Because somebody's paying him to be. It's as simple and transparent as that. Any idea who would be that keen to part with their cash?"

Konstantin could think of plenty of people who were less than fond of him, but to hire a hit man? "No," he said.

"Well you'd better work it out," said Sergey, "and quickly." He stood, threw some notes down on the table. "I'd better report this to my superiors. Come, I'll give you a lift back to your place."

"No thanks, I'll take the subway."

"Really?"

Konstantin nodded. "I've bought a ticket already, I wouldn't want to waste it."

Sergey shook his head in mock disappointment, said, "Stubborn bastard. Let me help though." He crooked a finger before Konstantin could protest. Sergey's bodyguards stood and came to their table.

"Give me your gun," said Sergey.

"Sir?"

"Don't make me repeat myself."

The bodyguard opened his mouth again, then thought better of it. He reached inside his jacket, tugged out an automatic, gave it to Sergey who slid it across the table to Konstantin.

"Magazines too," ordered Sergey. Two ended up in Konstantin's hand. "Here's my phone too."

Konstantin put his new possessions into pockets, said, "Thanks."

"If you make it, I'll be in touch. Watch your back, my friend."

Sergey stuck out a hand, they shook, and then he was gone.

Konstantin exited the restaurant, made his way through the throng of citizens and the odd tourist to the station. His eyes never stopped moving. Sergey's words juddered through his mind.

Only two things are important. The money and the conclusion.

He knew that when Shin came for him it would be a process that displayed meaning.

Sergey watched Konstantin turn a corner through the blacked out window. His gut told him something was going to happen to his comrade, and soon.

He turned to one of his bodyguards, said, "We'll head to his *yogwan*, just in case."

The bodyguard nodded, told the driver where to go.

"We've got weapons in the boot?" asked Sergey.

"Always."

"Good. I suspect we will need them. Pass me your mobile."

Konstantin trotted down several sets of stairs, felt the temperature rise another notch as the walls closed in. An odour assaulted his nostrils. Indescribable, but one that seemed to pervade every underground network the world over. Luck was with him because as he reached the platform a train arrived.

He climbed aboard, ignored the couple of empty seats and stood at the rear of the carriage. Back to the wall.

The journey was a series of lurching stops with a jerking acceleration in between. Konstantin waited for the doors to open before he moved from his position. Stepped onto the platform, waited there to see if anyone was following or watching him. In moments the narrow tiled area cleared of train and then people. Clear. He headed for the stairs.

The Russian entered the night air, albeit tainted with the slight whiff of a sewer. He walked slowly in the direction of his lodgings. Nothing out of the ordinary.

Which bothered the hell out of him.

The Yogwan

Sajik-dong Subdivision, Seoul

Mr. Lamb drew up a few blocks short of the *yogwan* where Hill had told him the Russian was staying. He'd driven around for a while getting a sense of the area. A little more for tourists than he'd have expected and plenty of students.

But ultimately Mr. Lamb shrugged it off. He didn't care why Boryakov had chosen his surroundings, just that he was *here*. He parked the car down a side street, one among many similar vehicles. Mr. Lamb leant against a wall in half-shadow, lit a cigarette and smoked it steadily. He saw and heard nothing immediate beyond the usual sounds of a city – traffic, people, animals.

He stayed at an angle against the brickwork for a few minutes, thinking. Knew that if he did this, completed treading the path he'd started out on two days ago, there would be no going back. Mr. Lamb was fully aware how it went against his morals, but he felt compelled to do so. Revenge, it was a powerful force.

He checked the gun in his pocket, the one Hill had provided, serial numbers filed off. It felt heavy, wrong. He rarely used weapons. But then again, this was an extraordinary moment.

Mr. Lamb took a deep breath, expelled the last of the nicotine fumes from his lungs, swore he'd never smoke again, stepped out of the gloom and towards brilliant light of retribution.

Shin observed Mr. Lamb. Watched the smoke plume into the air, detected the initial hesitance. Yet still he eventually moved forward.

Shin marvelled at how stupid British people were. The Empire was long gone, yet they acted like they still ruled the known world. It was clearly a trap, however Lamb entered its jaws with an arrogant swagger. The Russian, he was no better. Both born in countries that had once been great, but were now all but a laughing stock on the world stage.

And when Shin's plan came to fruition, so would be their respective so-called secret services. It was perfect, being paid by several parties to carry out the same task...

Konstantin climbed the stairs. Took them slowly. His senses niggled and picked at him. He knew they were nearby. Yet no one came close. Konstantin had given his opponents plenty of opportunities, both on the way to and returning from the restaurant. But still they left him alone. He didn't like it, preferred that things happened, and quickly.

Konstantin unlocked his door. It was exactly the same as when he'd left, although with one notable change.

The bodies sprawled across his mat.

Trust Thine Enemy

Konstantin had blood on his hands when the door opened behind him. He looked over his shoulder, saw Mr. Lamb standing in the gap, a gun protruding between knuckles so white they were alabaster. He watched eyes flick to the body, take everything in.

He ignored Lamb, went back to tending Hill, whose eyes were rolled back into his head, out of it with the shock. He pressed the towel harder against Hill's neck from where the blood seeped. A nick of the artery there. Just a small one. But enough for it to weep crimson in a steady, unstoppable flow. Hill's collar was soaked with it.

There was no point attending to the woman. She was already deceased. Had been for a while from the chill of her skin. Badly dyed hair and worse teeth. Bruises on her knees, cheekbone and upper arms. Track marks inside her elbow. Fresh as well as old. A prostitute most likely. She'd have been low rental at best. Maybe even free under the right circumstances.

"If you shoot me you'd better be ready to attend to your man here," said Konstantin.

Saw Mr. Lamb shift into his peripheral vision. Gun still up, held close to the body. Konstantin would have to leap to disarm him. But that would create two unwanted outcomes. One, Lamb would drill a bullet through the centre of Konstantin's heart within half a step. Two, it would mean taking the pressure off Hill's neck.

"You?" asked Mr. Lamb.

"No."

"It appears suspicious."

"It's supposed to. Look at the woman."

Mr. Lamb did so. Got in close, picked up on the blood that had pooled under her skin after death. Which meant she'd been stored somewhere before being brought to this room.

"And it wasn't me last time," said Konstantin. He felt Mr. Lamb stiffen. Knew he was taking a hell of a chance, but then again if Lamb didn't kill him, Shin would.

"Why should I believe you?" asked Mr. Lamb. He sounded incredibly calm for a man who'd lost everyone and everything close to him so recently.

Konstantin shrugged. Had nothing to prove and less to say.

"I came here to kill you," confessed Mr. Lamb.

"I know."

Hill coughed then. His eyes flickered open, focused on Konstantin. Hill gripped the Russian's hand, as if applying extra pressure to the towel himself would save him from death. He rolled his head towards Mr. Lamb. His eyes took a moment to focus, then lit up with a moment's clarity.

"They're outside," mumbled Hill. "Shin."

"None of us are supposed to get out of here alive," said Konstantin. "This has been the plan from the beginning, with its end here."

He stared at Mr. Lamb. Nothing flowed across the man's features. He looked cold, dead inside. The Russian didn't blame him.

"I could just kill you and get away."

Konstantin shook his head, said, "No."

"He's right," whispered Hill, his face creased with the effort. "They're everywhere."

"Who?" asked Lamb.

"I don't know. I thought I did, but I was wrong."

"Either we work together, or we're all dead," said Konstantin.

"I don't care," said Mr. Lamb.

"Me neither, but Hill here might."

Hill grinned weakly. Mr. Lamb lowered the gun, said, "What do you have in mind?"

The mobile in Konstantin's pocket rang then.

Evasion

Konstantin and Mr. Lamb moved once they heard the crump of explosions, one quickly on the heels of the other. Then shooting. The rattle of machine guns and the less frequent sound of handguns.

Konstantin rose from where he'd crouched, uncovered his ears, but they still rang. He nodded at Mr. Lamb, who responded with a minor inclination of his own. They stepped into the corridor, automatics up and in a slight crouch position.

They went in opposite directions. When Konstantin reached the corridor's culmination he knelt, peered around the corner, saw no one. Just doors to other guest rooms. He stood and trod carefully to the next intersection and repeated the process. Several bullets ripped into the plaster above his head.

The glimpse he'd obtained of the landing had revealed two men by the stairs. Their faces showed concern. The continued gunfire clearly wasn't part of the plan. He and Lamb would have to go through them to get out. Konstantin drew in a breath, whipped around the turn, trusted Mr. Lamb would be ready. He put two bullets into the guard nearest him. The man threw his arms up in the air, the shells punching holes in his chest. Konstantin drew a bead on the other local, but he was already down, put there by Mr. Lamb.

Konstantin stepped out from the angle and into the corridor, moved quickly across its width and took up position flat against the wall, the stairs to his right. Mr. Lamb held a similar station, nodded at Konstantin.

Konstantin rolled 180 degrees and fired off a burst upwards before he was able to fully form the thought that perhaps Mr. Lamb would leave him to be shot.

But no, his temporary ally followed through and loosed several bullets into the stairwell. Another nod and Konstantin placed a foot on the stairs, began to ascend, Mr. Lamb at his back.

Two flights up and they hit the roof.

Konstantin nudged the door open. He had to push hard as something was leaning against it. A body. With a black circle drilled neatly in the centre of its forehead.

"Someone got here before us," said Mr. Lamb.

Sergey.

Konstantin crossed to the edge of the roof, looked down. Plenty of flashing lights as the emergency services appeared. Police and ambulances. The latter for Hill. He knew Sergey would be down there somewhere.

"I expect Shin escaped," said Mr. Lamb.

"More than likely."

"We've still got some business to attend to."

"Agreed."

Konstantin shifted away from the precipice, dropped his weapon onto the floor. He took up a fighting stance, fists raised to chest height. Mr. Lamb emulated the Russian. Took a step forward then.

Close contact.

Shocked Shin

Shin drove away from the scene. His heart screamed at him to return, to finish the job, but his head had control. Better to escape than be captured or killed. There would have to be another day to complete the job. He'd been paid, after all...

Back From The Dead

Thirty Six Hours Later
Regent's Park, London

Dennis sat on the same bench he had every day since he'd started at MI6. The summer continued to be spectacular, but he barely felt the sun on his face. Instead he focused on a man who shouldn't be here. One who should have never made it out of South Korea.

Mr. Lamb sat on the opposite end of the bench. He looked battered and bruised. Dennis dreaded to think what the other guy looked like.

"Good to see you," said Dennis, his tone impassive.

Mr. Lamb didn't reply. Merely turned his coal black pupils onto Dennis, who shuddered.

"We have plenty to discuss," said Mr. Lamb.

Dennis nodded slowly.

A
Chorus
Of
Bells

No Refuge For The Wicked

7.00pm, Christmas Eve

Even the church was noisy.

Is there nowhere I can get peace? Konstantin wondered to himself. Too noisy at home so he'd ventured out.

Konstantin wasn't a religious man, he was simply here in an attempt to escape the clamour of celebration. Christmas cheer was upon Margate, but the tramp wanted no part of it. Although churches were supposed to be a source of refuge, they had the added benefit of possessing some spectacular architecture or interesting interred people to admire.

He felt comfortable in places of the dead, couldn't explain why. Graveyards in particular, but the winos took all the benches at night and Konstantin wasn't that desperate.

The Russian occupied a pew of well-polished wood, tough on the backside. Not a cushion in sight. Suffering for a God he didn't recognise, at the rear of the nave as far as possible from the altar. Away from the eyes of Christ crucified on the cross from which he hung.

The church was a hive of activity. An army of old ladies buzzing up and down the aisle, readying the place of worship for precisely that activity. Stands of flowers were being placed at the end of each row of pews, sweeping, tidying up. The priest was practising his sermon in the pulpit, muttering to himself, waving his hands to emphasise relevant points. Konstantin figured there must be many to make because his limbs barely stopped moving, other than to turn the paper over to read the next words he'd scrawled.

But his attempt at solitude was a spectacular failure. One of the cleaning brigade was polishing the pews, she'd be on him soon. He sighed, decided there was somewhere else that may better suit his purpose. Rose up, winced at the ache in his posterior.

The not so penitent man left.

Pick Up

7.10pm, Christmas Eve

"There he is," said the driver, nodded towards the man exiting the church. Light reflected in equal proportions off his glasses and bald head. "Let's go."

The very fat man sat next to him wheezed, as if speaking was a huge effort, said, "I'll be glad when this is over, then we can go down the pub."

"You need to lay off the alcohol."

"Why?"

"It's high in calories."

"And that's relevant to me because…?"

Tam, the driver, opened his mouth to speak, shut it again. It was a conversation he and Wallace had many times. Too many.

"Come on," he said. "Let's get it done.

Picking up the guy was surprisingly straightforward. Tam distracted him with the sight of a sharp knife while Wallace literally struck. Tam got the unconscious man's shoulders, Wallace his feet, as usual. Threw the unconscious form into the boot none too gently, bound his wrists with a plastic cable tie. Tam didn't want any hassle when the guy woke up. Life was too short for hassle. Wallace slammed the boot lid down, waddled to the passenger side while Tam made the call.

"We've got him, Ambrus," he said.

"Good. Now deal with him. I don't want to see his face around again."

"Okay," said Tam, but he was speaking to the ether, Ambrus had already disconnected, proving to Tam yet again that the Hungarian was as rude as he was illegal.

He got into the Merc, twisted the key to match the expression on his face.

Yuletide Cheer

Konstantin sat in the shadow of an artwork, stared with the shell lady out to sea. Felt as cold and lifeless as she. Barely felt the chill through the grubby fabric of his green-ish coat.

Even at the end of the harbour arm, the waves battering its base, the wind battering him, his heart battering his chest, Konstantin Boryakov could at times clearly hear the revelry as if he were in its midst.

Sometimes the high wind kept it at bay, others it was as clear as day. Like a door opening and closing. Blocking the sound, then releasing it. Mostly he heard high-pitched shrieks of laughter, cheers, singing. Even the faint sound of church bells, calling what few worshippers were left into its dank interior, but he'd just left there and wouldn't be going back.

And beneath it all an undercurrent of throbbing music that he didn't tap his fingers to spilled out from the pubs and clubs. The usual fare, only played at this time of the year. In about thirty hours' time these particular tracks would be packed away to repose for another three hundred and odd days, until the next time they were metaphorically dusted off for their next annual outing.

He didn't hate Christmas, far from it. But times like these were best shared with others. And Konstantin had no one. Not any more. His daughter lived nearby, not that she knew about him, but Konstantin wouldn't, couldn't intrude. Because he was dead. To his family at least.

Instead he simply watched, from a distance, invisible in his disguise. Made sure she got through life with as few knocks and scrapes as possible. Which, he consoled himself, was much more than the average father who worked eight hours a day in an office was able, and often willing, to do.

However, even in the midst of cheer bad things happened. The tramp looked over his shoulder as something unexpected intruded. A white light bathed him momentarily. Not an angel from above, because those sorts of visitations don't happen, for there is nothing before or after life. Konstantin believed that when we are gone, we are gone. He'd seen the life go out in too many people's eyes to think otherwise.

No, this was the harsh tungsten glare of car headlights. It had swung onto the harbour arm, the concrete strip which jutted out of the waves to protect the anchorage from the worst of the elements, and then coasted past the line of a low buildings, all currently unoccupied and dark. The Merc was brought up short by bollards, small, but tightly spaced enough to block the vehicle's progress.

The engine died, but the beams remained strong. Konstantin held himself as still as the statue. Then the lights followed the engine and perished. The tramp took his chance to shift himself then, into the shadow of one of the doorways. Ignored the smell of piss. Knew the car's occupants wouldn't see him. Dark clothes, huge beard helped him merge into the blackness.

The driver's door popped then, weakly illuminating the interior of the car with a low wattage bulb. The driver stepped out, stood upright. Bald cranium and excessive height was all Konstantin could get at this distance. Seconds later the passenger side opened up too, although the driver's companion took considerably longer to exit, with huffing and puffing as audible as the Christmas celebrations. The guy was huge, vastly overweight, looked like a well stuffed tent.

The follicly challenged guy took a moment to check out the immediate surroundings. Stared slowly all around him, brief flicker of light off the glasses he wore. Then stalked towards the sea. Reached the shell lady, touched her momentarily, brushed his fingertips along the surface. Then to the rear of the building. Konstantin heard him trot up the steps that led onto its roof.

Evidently satisfied they were alone, he returned to the rear of the car, had the boot open and all in the time it took his fat friend to waddle over and join him. A patient and particular man, then.

The tall guy leaned into the boot space, heaved something out. Konstantin heard it slap onto the concrete. Had weight to it, but was soft. Like a sack of potatoes. Could see enough from the angle he was at to know it was a body, though. It'd been taking a ride in the space normal people placed their luggage.

It wasn't a corpse, for after a couple of moments the fat guy pulled the individual up by its hair. Small and skinny, short hair. Must have made some sort of comment as the fat guy snarled, hammered a fist into his gut. Made him double over with a whoosh of expelled air. Sound of retching moments later. Wouldn't be the only person puking up in Margate tonight, that was for sure.

"We haven't got time for this, Wallace," said the tall guy, broad Glaswegian accent carried on the wind. Razor blades and cricket bats. "Quit fucking around."

Fat man fixed his colleague with a hard stare, but yanked the captive up by a hand under his armpit.

"All right Tam, cool your fucking jets, okay?" Same inflection to his words.

They walked the guy on, one either side, guards escorting a prisoner. His head was down, feet dragging on the rough surface. Reluctant to make the journey.

He was shorter even than Wallace, by a good head. Konstantin caught the pale face, then caught a flash of white at the neck. Frowned, couldn't believe what his eyes were telling him even as the short man looked back over his shoulder.

"Don't bother looking. No one's coming to save you, Teddy. It's just us and the waves."

A Bad Man Gets A Good Kicking

7.20pm Christmas Eve

Once the trio were out of sight, Konstantin had a choice to make.

Help, or leave well alone?

This wasn't his problem, but then neither had all the others he'd managed to get himself embroiled in. But it was Christmas Eve. And the dog collar at the priest's throat made an impact on Konstantin. One he struggled to ignore.

Decided to make it a New Year's resolution to stay out of business that wasn't his. But January was eight days away.

He slid out of the doorway, kept his back to the wall, body in gloom. Once around the corner he was literally exposed. The wind picked at his clothes, spray from the battering waves splattered his face and there was light. No more shadows to skulk within. But it didn't matter because the two guys had their attention focused on their captive, backs to Konstantin.

While Wallace held Teddy's arms in a tight grip, Tam pulled on a pair of black gloves.

"You don't need to do this," said the priest.

"Too late Teddy. You had twenty four hours to clear off. That's come and gone. Ambrus is pissed off with you. And that's something we have to put right."

"I couldn't leave."

"Why?"

"Nowhere to go."

"There's always somewhere when the other option is dying."

"Look, I'll leave her alone. You'll have no more trouble from me."

"Yeah, yeah. Heard it all before, haven't we Wallace? Always amazes me when you lot take a fancy to a tart."

"It's Christmas. Time of hope and goodwill to all men?"

"Not fucking likely, pal."

The fat guy grunted, seemed to just want to get on with it. Confirmed Konstantin's view with a sharp comment.

"You're right Wallace," said Tam, and stuck a fist into Teddy's solar plexus before the priest could say another word.

Wallace hung onto Teddy as he doubled over, the second time in a couple of minutes.

Tam knelt down, grasped Teddy's chin between two long fingers, tugged his head up so their eyes met.

"Now this can either go the long road, or the short road. It's up to you. Either way, it's a good kicking, then a swim. The water's freezing so you'll not feel it for long."

Wallace snorted, clearly enjoying himself.

"You'd do this to a man of the cloth?" Teddy squeezed the words out between gasps.

That really made the pair laugh.

"Nobody believes in God any more," said Tam. "Even priests."

Tam stood, with a wave of his hand indicated that Wallace was to pull Teddy to his feet. Once upright, Tam raised a fist, but stopped short, said, "What the fuck?"

"Spare change?" repeated Konstantin, a slur smeared thickly across his voice. He staggered out of the shadows, palm held out.

"If you know what's good for you, you'll fuck right off old man. Now."

"For Christmas drink, my friend."

"Just get rid of him," said Wallace, shook his head. "He's pissed, won't remember a thing in the morning. And if he does, who's going to listen to a tramp?"

Tam dug around in his pocket, said, "I haven't got any money."

Konstantin turned to Wallace, who repeated the search for cash, taking one hand off Teddy in the process. Found a few coins, tossed them in Konstantin's general direction.

Konstantin made to bend over, took his chance then. Sprinted across the short gap, planted a heavy fist on the Tam's jaw, who went down fast. Before his head smacked on the concrete, Konstantin pivoted ninety degrees, swung a boot into Wallace's knee. Heard it crack.

The big guy screamed, let go of Teddy as his excessive weight shifted onto his other limb, which couldn't take the extra load. Wallace followed Tam onto the floor. Ridiculously easy.

Teddy looked at the damage, appeared unmoved by it. "Hey, thanks," he said. "Can you get these off me?" Held his hands out, wrists had been bound with tie wraps.

Konstantin shook his head. "No knife." Didn't carry them, people that did so were usually nutters.

"Ah, fuck it," said the priest. "He's got one." Kicked Tam to indicate who he meant.

Konstantin searched Tam, pulled out a knife with a small, but wicked blade. Cut the ties off. Teddy rubbed at his wrists. Knelt down next to Wallace, whose screams had subsided to pained moans.

"Help me! My fucking knee!" he said. "It's agony!"

"You were going to do worse to me, you fat bastard. Tell me where I can find her."

"No! I can't!"

"If you do I'll get you to a hospital."

Wallace shook his head.

"Okay then."

Teddy pushed himself upright again, Konstantin was taken by surprise when the priest started kicking Wallace. It didn't seem like something a member of the clergy should be doing, but he had grown up in Russia. It would be like putting the boot into a whale, all that blubber soaking up the impact. Teddy turned his attention to Wallace's knee. Pressed his foot against the damaged joint. Wallace screamed.

"Okay, I'll tell you!"

Konstantin put an arm out, grabbed the priest, pulled him away. The small man was panting slightly at the effort.

"Where is she?"

"At work."

Teddy leapt up and, before Konstantin could stop him, rolled Wallace like a barrel and within moments had him in the water with a huge splash. Tam was a simpler process. Teddy dragged him by an ankle, then nudged him into the water with a foot.

Teddy shrugged, said, "Fair's fair. They were going to do it to me."

Konstantin shrugged. Had no sympathy for the pair. He started to walk away. New Year's resolution and all that.

"Wait, you can't leave me," shouted Teddy.

"Why?"

Teddy didn't say anything, seemed not to have an immediate answer. Eventually, "It's Christmas?"

"Why does everyone keep saying that?"

"Because it's true. I need your help."

Konstantin sighed.

They were off the harbour arm and into the Old Town before the shakes punched into Teddy. So bad he had to flop down onto a kerb. Wrapped his arms around his body like he was freezing to death. Konstantin could hear the priest's teeth rattle in his skull.

"You okay?" asked Konstantin.

"Never better," said the priest. Threw a sliver of a grin the tramp's way from where he sat. Unconvincing.

Then, moments later, Teddy began to laugh. A low chuckle that developed into gut bursting mirth where he could barely draw breath. He drew strange looks from passers-by. The tramp and the priest together. Although who was saving who?

Konstantin let Teddy subside, eventually said, "There's somewhere we should go."

Where No One Knows Your Name

7.35pm Christmas Eve

"You're not fucking coming in here. No way," said Dick, the landlord of Konstantin's local boozer. Well, only boozer.

He wouldn't, couldn't go anywhere else. No other pub would let him through its doors without a serious altercation. Not that Konstantin minded a fight, quite the opposite. Sometimes a dust-up was essential, like others needed sex to relieve tension.

Just not today.

On the way here Konstantin had discarded his green-ish coat, too many questions to answer should he enter Dick's pub wearing it.

Konstantin had a number of places around town that he could use in an emergency. A garage, warehouse unit, disused shop among others. With stuff in it should he be in trouble. Weapons. Medical equipment. Clothes. He hadn't wanted to take the priest back to his house. Didn't like anyone knowing about his other life.

Even the retreats had to remain uncompromised, so he left Teddy on a corner a few streets away in the shadows. The priest had suggested standing under a light, claimed it was safer that way. But Konstantin knew better. Managed to refrain from rolling his eyeballs. Didn't bother to explain that if the local scallies caught sight of him they'd strip him bare, metaphorically speaking. Like parking your car in view, just shows the thugs what they can have away. Naïve.

So Konstantin pushed him into the shadows, ignored the priest's protests. Looked over his shoulder as he walked away, swore he could see Teddy's wide eyes shining out like beacons. Quickly changed into a black leather jacket, tied his hair back and had a quick wash so he didn't look, or smell, grimy.

He hated being called Dick, but everyone did, because he was. Tall, but stooped so he wouldn't stand out. Dyed what was left of his thinning hair, bit of a stomach on him. The guy was a bully when he had the opportunity, used his apparent authority to give people a hard time.

"I've told you before. No foreigners, no women, no religious fanatics. They're all fucking trouble, every last one of them."

Dick had no idea Konstantin was Russian because he kept his accent under wraps when in most company.

Konstantin turned to Teddy. Plucked the dog collar from his neck. Dropped it on the floor. Teddy scooped the once-white band up, stuffed it in his pocket.

"Satisfied?" said Konstantin. Towered over Dick.

To be fair the landlord stood his ground, said, "No. Doesn't change the fact he's a God botherer."

Konstantin sighed. Looked around the dingy pub. Sticky floor, wet tables and rickety stools. Even the dim lighting couldn't hide the fact that this was the crappest watering hole in Margate and that Konstantin could easily make it look far, far worse.

"Are you sure you want to do this?" he said.

Dick looked into the tramp's eyes. The landlord gulped, took a step back, said, "I've only just reopened after the last time."

"Then get us a drink and you won't be closed again."

Dick looked from Teddy to Konstantin, then around the largely empty pub.

He stepped back to bar, leant over it, whispered, "Can we keep this between ourselves? Don't want my reputation ruined."

The Russian almost laughed, amused that Dick felt he had a status to protect. It couldn't get any worse. Universally loathed and distrusted. Routinely threw around his miniscule authority, but ran away when there was any serious confrontation. No one Konstantin knew had a good word to say about the guy.

"Okay," he agreed. "Your secret's safe with us." Managed to avoid a conspiratorial wink.

Dick bared his rotting teeth in an approximation of a smile. "Usual?"

"Make it two."

Dick turned to the optics, measured out the vodkas. No ice, no water to dilute the alcohol and its kick. Placed the glasses on the tacky wooden surface. Held his hand out for payment.

"Put it on my tab," said Konstantin. Turned away before Dick could argue.

Led Teddy to a table as far away from the landlord as possible. There weren't any frills in Dick's place. A fruit machine was as far as it went. Konstantin stayed away from this too, didn't want anyone stood at his shoulder. Otherwise, no music, no television. What you mostly got instead was a wildly coloured carpet, strong alcohol and peace. And no reference to Christmas, it being a religious festival. The pub looked the same all year round, unless there was a royal event on. Then you couldn't move for red, white and blue. No question regarding Dick's patriotism, although just about every other facet of the man was dubious.

The place was quiet. No voices to fill the air. The few people present sat by themselves, lost in the isolation of self-loathing and alcohol. Tiny Al nodded at Konstantin from the fruit machine.

Konstantin pushed one of the glasses over to Teddy.

"I don't partake," he said. "Against my religion."

Konstantin seriously doubted Teddy had any religion but said, "For your nerves."

Teddy lifted the tumbler to his lips, his hand shook. Konstantin heard the glass rattle against his teeth. Teddy gulped the fiery fluid down in a couple of goes. Coughed. Wiped his mouth with the back of his skinny digits. Konstantin threw his own glass back, barely felt the liquid's descent. Turned to Dick, three fingers raised. Ignored the landlord's grimace.

"So, what's going on with you?" said Konstantin.

"Nothing."

Konstantin knew it was a lie, said, "A couple of guys put you into the boot of a car. They're going to kick the crap out of you and throw you into the sea. That doesn't happen for nothing. For those people, time is money."

Dick delivered the next round of vodka. Konstantin nodded his thanks. The landlord stalked away. Looked like he'd sucked on a lemon.

The Russian pushed a glass at Teddy.

"I still don't drink," he said.

"You do tonight. It'll help calm you down."

The priest shook his head, but resistance was minimal. Sank the next shot. Konstantin noticed the tremor was subsiding. Sat back. Let the alcohol and the silence take their toll.

A couple of lads entered the bar, shattered the silence with shouts and laughter. Students probably, from their cultured scruffiness. Clearly spent too long getting the right side of shabby. Four of them stood on the threshold, like they couldn't go any further. Scanned the interior, saw Dick put two hands on the bar, lean forward and hunch his shoulders. They backed out.

Dick turned away, shook his head. Konstantin was surprised he'd managed to unpeel his palms without leaving a layer of skin behind.

"There's a woman. That's why they were going to kill me."

"Sounds like a bit of an over-reaction."

"She's tied up with some nasty people. They won't let me have her."

Konstantin grimaced, he'd heard enough. Love. Always complicating life. He wanted no part of it.

"It's not like that," said Teddy hurriedly. Must have caught the look on the tramp's face. "She's stuck. She's a prostitute."

"Perhaps you'd better explain," said Konstantin.

Tam Parts The Waves

7.45pm Christmas Eve

Tam staggered through the surf. Managed to get a few feet above the high water mark, half in, half out the water. Waves lapped at his legs in an apparent attempt to reclaim him.

He heaved in lungfuls of salty air. Rolled onto his side and retched. A plume of seawater and bile splashed over him and the sand. He didn't care, just couldn't believe his luck that he was still alive. Wondered if Wallace had made it too, but knew deep down there was little chance of it. The last time he'd glimpsed Wallace he was floating face down, floundering in the waves like a ship that had lost power. The guy could barely walk down the stairs without having a coronary, never mind swim for hundreds of yards against a swift current.

The Scot rolled onto his back, stared at the stars a moment. Amazed at their beauty. Their timelessness. Even though they were blurry. His glasses had been washed off his face. Right then Tam swore to himself that when this was over he was pursuing the good things in life.

Just not yet. One more thing to do first. He got onto all fours. Pushed himself onto his haunches, then rose. Like the oldest man in the world. Worn out. Seaweed hung off him, but Tam didn't care. Felt in his pockets, no mobile either. Began to make his way up the beach. Had to get to a payphone. Warn Ambrus.

Then he'd get the train back to Glasgow. Leave these mad bastards to it.

The Knocking Shop

8.00pm Christmas Eve

"That's where she works," said Teddy. Pointed at a tall, terraced building. One street back and parallel to the seafront. Many floors. Unlike its neighbours, not split into multiple flats. Which made it highly unusual. Once, there had apparently been hundreds of hotels and guest houses in Margate. But one after the other they'd all closed, had been turned to flats and hostels for the afflicted and disaffected who sponged off the taxpaying employed.

"How many?" said Konstantin, counted off the floors and windows.

"Girls?"

The tramp nodded.

"Hard to say. Ten, twelve maybe."

The front door opened a crack. Revealed a furtive, short man who stepped outside, tugged a flat cap low down over his eyes and a coat about his body. Hard to distinguish anything about him. Konstantin drew Teddy deeper into the shadows of the narrow, rubbish strewn alley. Heard the man's rapid footsteps as he disappeared.

No sooner had the short man gone, than another arrived. Rapped at the door, slid inside. The click of locks carried easily to where they hid.

"Put your collar back on," said Konstantin. "We need your trusting face."

An old woman stood on the step, quizzical look on her features which softened as soon as she saw Teddy's persuasion. Lined so deeply there were probably lost tribes somewhere at their base.

"Can I help you?" she said.

"I hope so," said Konstantin.

"Is it about them across the road?"

Mrs. Faith, Gwen to her friends apparently, poured tea through a strainer into a china teacup, said, "Milk? Sugar?"

"Just milk, thanks," Teddy replied. They were seated at a small table in the centre of a high ceilinged room. Large windows took up most of one wall. They had a perfect view of the street below. The binoculars on the sill helped too.

She poured in an excessive amount of the white liquid, handed the cup over. Repeated the process with Konstantin. He hated tea, only drank coffee, but didn't want to offend the woman.

"Are you with the police?" she asked.

"Would you like us to be?" said Konstantin.

"No, they've been utterly useless so far. I've reported the goings on over there time and again. The men in blue look at me like they should be dressed in white and carting me off to a mental hospital."

"We are not representatives of the law," said Teddy. "Only God."

Konstantin fought to hold from rolling his eyes. Stuck to sighing.

"I don't mind who you're with, love, as long as you deal with that bunch of shites."

"Would you mind telling us what goes on?"

"Well, everything. Telling you what doesn't happen would probably take less time, love. There's men coming and going all hours of the day and night. Using the prostitutes, poor girls."

"Do you know any of them?" said Teddy. His voice had softened, like he was taking confession.

"I used to speak to one or two, when they were allowed outside. That hasn't happened for a while, mind. Hungarian girls mostly. Told they were coming here for a better life and now spend most of it on their backs being sweated and pawed over by grubby men."

"When did they stop the girls going out?"

"A few months ago. Probably my fault. I went to the Police; suddenly the activity over there becomes less visible. Like they knew they were being watched."

"Someone on the inside?" said Teddy.

"Possible," said Konstantin.

"I didn't give up though," said Gwen. "I started taking pictures."

Telephone Man

8.05pm Christmas Eve

Finally. A fucking phone that hadn't been vandalised. Tam couldn't believe it. Stepped inside the box. The interior absolutely reeked of piss. Some tramp's toilet most likely. Perhaps even that fucker who'd hit him.

He spent a moment perusing the cards stuck to the walls. Girls and a few guys offering a shockingly wide array of services.

Then remembered what he had to do. Picked up the receiver. Had no money, so called collect. Got through. Struggled to understand what Ambrus was saying. Bloody accent was impossible to understand down the wire. Another reason to fuck off home. Get back to his own people.

"You what pal?" said Tam.

Ambrus sighed, sounded like an icy wind in his ear, then said, "Go to house."

"Why? Teddy won't turn up. Doesn't have the balls."

"I need someone I trust to look after place 'til I arrive. You nearer than me."

Tam's turn to sigh, "Okay."

Ambrus disconnected.

Tam considered going to the train station, something would be along to whisk him away. But if he disobeyed Ambrus and was caught? Incredibly dangerous.

So he got walking.

Mugshots

8.10pm Christmas Eve

"My grandson set all this up for me," she said, manipulating a mouse to bring up some well-known photographic software. Besides the PC, Gwen owned a printer and a digital SLR camera with a long lens which perched on a tripod to stare through the window. "It'll let me take video too."

She entered the directory, several folders within marked 'Clients', 'Associates', 'Girls' and 'Uncategorised'.

"You're in here," she said, tapped the latter folder on the screen. "I'll delete you now I know you're on the side of the angels."

"One of us is," said Konstantin.

"Oh no, I've been around long enough to recognise good from evil."

Konstantin wasn't sure how to take that, decided it wisest to move on.

"Who are the associates?"

"They're the people that run the girls," said Gwen. Double clicked the mouse. Minimised photos popped onto the screen.

"These two show up a lot," said Gwen.

"We've met," said Konstantin.

Tam and Wallace.

"Lucky you."

"And this pair." One black and wide, the other white and feral.

"Jasper and Eric," said Teddy.

Gwen moved on. Another couple of clicks.

"These seem to be the ones in charge," she said. Four men, one woman. "But him," Gwen tapped the screen, "he's the man. Hungarian, like the girls. I don't know his name, sorry."

"That's Ambrus," said Teddy.

Konstantin peered at him. Grey haired, small beard, distinguished looking. Had a phone pressed to his ear, looking off into the distance.

"And the woman?" Unusual for a female to be involved at the business end.

"His girlfriend."

Konstantin stood, wrote down a number. Asked Gwen to call it in five minutes.

He was out of the flat and in the street before either Gwen or Teddy could protest. He expected they were watching him as he crossed the street, that if he looked up now the old woman would have him in her camera lens.

The door was opening as he reached it, yet another punter making his escape. Konstantin barely glanced at him. Got halfway inside before a hand landed on his chest. It belonged to a huge black guy. Barrel chested. More fat than muscle, more imposition than proposition. This would be Jasper. Another guy behind. Pointed nose, protruding teeth. Eric.

Hard to see inside. Dim, like they were in a cave or downstairs in a club.

"Who are you, mate?" asked Jasper. "This is an invite only facility."

"Paul," said Konstantin, "someone told me about your place."

"Uh-huh. Name?"

"Tam. Scottish fella I met in a pub recently."

Jasper sighed, "For fuck's sake, sounds like the sort of thing that wanker would do."

"You going to let me in, or what?"

Jasper looked over his shoulder. Eric shrugged, said, "Slow night, why not?"

The black guy nodded for Konstantin to enter. Once inside he looked around. A narrow corridor, painted some bland colour. A couple of lights which threw out weak beams. Plain carpet. Closed doors periodically along its length.

Jasper said, "Okay. Arms up. We've got to search you first."

Konstantin did as he was told.

Confessional

8.20pm Christmas Eve

Teddy didn't realise he'd been holding his breath until stars pirouetted in front of his eyes. He expelled the carbon dioxide laden air in a huge huff as Konstantin entered the den.

"I was doing the same," said Gwen. "I've been desperate for someone to deal with them, but now it's happening..."

"Yes."

Silence descended again. No movement in the street.

"I'd like to come and see you when this is over. Perhaps listen to your message. You clearly care for people."

"Just one person really." Teddy went bright red as soon as he said it, saw Gwen's knowing look. Felt he had to confess. "She used to come into the church, sit at the back and listen to the sermons. Other times just stare at the altar when the place was empty. Always in the same seat. Eventually I struck up the courage to talk to her. She was fascinating. So much to say. But so much sadness. Then one day she just stopped coming."

"How did you know where she 'worked'?"

Teddy felt another rush of embarrassment. Gwen seemed to know how to get to the depths of his soul.

"I followed her one day," he said in a barely audible tone.

"How long have you been a man of the cloth?" asked Gwen.

"A while now," said Teddy.

"Where do you preach?"

"Nearby. It's only a small church. You wouldn't know it."

"Try me."

Teddy sighed, peeled his eyes off the house opposite to look at Gwen. Decided she'd only stop once he'd answered.

"Saint Augustine's."

Teddy put his eyes back to the binoculars, pleased she seemed to have swallowed the story. But his heart hit the

249

back of his throat when she said, "There isn't a church called Saint Augustine's."

"Ah." He put the binoculars down.

"I'll make another cup of tea, then you can tell me all about it."

"Do you have a bathroom I can use?" said Teddy. He suddenly felt rather ill.

Tam turned into the road. Felt dwarfed by the tall buildings that stretched up into the night sky.

He'd had a few odd looks on the long walk over. He was still dripping wet, what little hair he had plastered to his forehead. At least he'd got rid of the seaweed now. That seemed to be the main reason for people to raise his eyebrows at him. Looked like some dodgy version of King Canute. But this was a place used to the outlandish – he'd been ignored after an initial glance. A mental shrug that dismissed him.

Tam still couldn't remember what had brought him here, but tomorrow, perhaps even tonight, he'd be on the first train to London that he could catch. Half a day and he'd be back where he belonged.

A few yards and he reached the front door of the knocking shop. Wasn't his sort of thing, but it paid the bills, so he wasn't going to criticise the patrons.

He had a key, but knocked anyway, didn't want to cause Jasper any offence. He protected his little domain with a glare. And if that didn't work, then fists the size of an average man's head usually would suffice. Worse was that fucking lunatic, Eric. The one with the knife. Something distasteful about him.

No answer. That was a surprise. Knocked again, waited. Patience wasn't something Tam commonly exhibited, so he dug around in a sodden pocket for his key...

Teddy wiped his mouth with the back of his hand, flushed the toilet. Found some spray to mask the vomit smell and mouthwash to disinfect his tongue.

"Sorry about that," he said. Then he saw Gwen's face. She was at the window, binoculars in hand. "What's the matter?"

Slash

8.20pm Christmas Eve

Konstantin hit Jasper first. Took him completely by surprise. That's the trouble with being bigger than everyone else, it provides a false sense of security. Konstantin ruthlessly exploited this fact. As Jasper had come in for the pat-down, Konstantin kneed him in the bollocks. Doesn't matter who you are, a solid impact in the soft parts is going to put anyone down.

Jasper sagged to his knees, Konstantin thudded a fist into his nose. Felt the bone crack, warm liquid splash his knuckles. Eyes rolled back in his head, toppled backwards. Switched his attention to Eric before the black guy kissed the floor.

Eric hadn't twitched, but then some primal part of his brain must have clicked because he reached inside his jacket, pulled out a knife. The blade emerged with a click. It looked sharp enough to cut the air. The little guy grinned a grin as wicked as the blade he held.

"Yeah, you wanna be afraid, old man," said Eric. "I'm going to carve you into tiny pieces and feed you to the gulls."

He stepped forward, favoured his left leg as if he were fencing, huge smile on his face. Held the knife up at chest height, the point aiming at Konstantin's chest. He rushed forward, slashed. Konstantin heard a high pitched whistle as the knife sliced the space an inch in front of him.

Eric repeated his attack, Konstantin guessed the aim was to drive him backwards down the corridor until he was unable to retreat any further.

A third swipe and Konstantin made his move, feinted a stumble to his right, away from the knife. Eric rushed forward, came in close. Konstantin grabbed his wrist. The younger man tried to force the knife on, but Konstantin was far stronger. Pushed Eric backwards until he hit a wall. Now it was he who had nowhere to go. The grin tumbled. Konstantin slowly forced his arm back, twisted the knife so it

251

pointed at its owner. Kept inching the blade towards his attacker's stomach.

"No, please," Eric pleaded.

Konstantin ignored him, anyone who intended the Russian harm received it in kind. He kept up the pressure until the knife pierced Eric's skin, pushed into the gut. He screamed. Still Konstantin pushed until the point hit the wall.

Eric stopped struggling. One last sour breath escaped his lips as Konstantin released his grip and the body slipped to the floor. Konstantin left the weapon embedded, he didn't like knives. Used by maniacs. One less now.

The black guy began to groan then. Konstantin stepped over Eric, hit Jasper hard on the jaw. The noise stopped.

Then the doorbell rang.

Teddy To The Rescue

8.21pm Christmas Eve

"What shall we do?" said Teddy.

"There's not much I'm able to," said Gwen, "I'm 83."

"Shit. I have to do something."

"I'll call the police."

Teddy turned away from the window, shook his head, said, "No, everyone inside will be arrested. I'll never see her again."

"Time to be a hero then," said Gwen.

Teddy gulped.

"Take this," she said. Cold metal pressed into his palm.

Teddy's Reward

8.25pm Christmas Eve

Konstantin ignored the knock, went down the corridor and tried the first door. It swung open silently. Revealed a small room full of junk. Went back into hall, got his hands under knife boy's armpits. Dragged him the short distance, left a thin trail of blood.

Another knock, harder this time. Konstantin resisted the urge to look through the peephole. Dragged Jasper by the ankles, had to lean back at a steep angle to get sufficient leverage to get him moving.

As he re-entered the corridor, the front door swung back on its hinges.

Tam.

"Oh fuck," he said.

Konstantin strode forward, grabbed a bunch of Tam's sodden jacket, yanked him over the step. Kicked the door to behind him.

"Look man, I don't want any trouble!" said Tam.

"Then why are you here?"

"I'm soaking, nowhere else to go and dry off," lied Tam. Looked past Konstantin, gulped when he saw a crimson stain. "Where are the guys?"

"Your friends?"

Tam shrugged.

"They're dead."

The Scot pulled his eyes off the gore and stared into Konstantin's face.

"Why are you here?" repeated Konstantin.

"My boss is coming."

"When?"

"Any time. You should go, he's a killer."

"No problem. So am I."

At that moment Teddy burst in, a poker raised above his head. He looked from Konstantin to Tam and back again.

"You've got it under control then," he said. Let his arm and the poker sag.

"For now. The big man is on his way."

"Gwen's calling the number you gave her."

"Then we'd better get a move on." Turned to Teddy. "What's her name?"

"Eh?"

"Your girl. That's why we're here."

"What are you, a mind reader?"

Konstantin shook his head, said, "People reader."

"Look, as pleasant as all this is," said Tam, "I'd like to get the fuck out of here. Please."

"Go," said Konstantin.

Tam turned and bolted out the open door.

"Room five," said Teddy.

Up two flights of narrow stairs, threadbare carpet, more magnolia walls. A plain door, chipped white paint.

Teddy opened the door, stuck his head in. Konstantin waited outside. A minute later Teddy emerged with a blonde waif, skinnier than a guitar string, heavy lipstick. Huge grin plastered on his face.

"She said yes!"

"Leaving town?"

Teddy nodded.

"Take these," said Konstantin.

It's Over

9.00pm Christmas Eve

Ambrus fumed silently, invisible behind blacked out windows. From the comfort of his car parked a hundred yards up the street, watched the cops raid one of his most lucrative business ventures. Vowed to find out who'd given him the problem and didn't care how long it took.

"Let's go," he told his driver.

Gwen smiled as she watched the girls being brought out of the flat. Before she went downstairs to talk to the policeman called Gregory she'd been told to call, she deleted all the photos of the priest and his large friend. No need for anyone to know who'd been involved.

They were in the Merc. Teddy driving, the now ex-prostitute in the passenger seat. Through town. People milled everywhere. Mostly drunk. Took longer than expected to get along the seafront. Looked like half the drivers were pissed too. Weaving cars, blowing horns. The occupants of the Merc sat calmly, waiting for the alcoholic storm to pass by.

"Where do we go?" asked the girl.

"Far away."

Ho Ho Ho

12.05am Christmas Day

Konstantin sat at the rear of the church. Listened to the midnight mass. A single face in a sea of many. But just this once he didn't feel so alone. Lifted the hymn sheet up so he could see it better in the candlelight. Wished a mental happy Christmas to his family.

Sang at the top of his lungs.

Lightning Source UK Ltd.
Milton Keynes UK
UKOW02f2347071216
289467UK00004B/348/P